Flawed

The Mechanical Trilogy, Book 3

by

Pauline C. Harris

F & I
by Melange Books

Published by
Fire and Ice
A Young Adult Imprint of Melange Books, LLC
White Bear Lake, MN 55110
www.fireandiceya.com

ISBN: 978-1-61235-734-8 Print

Cover Art by Caroline Andrus

Flawed
Pauline C. Harris

With Yvonne in control, Michael perfected, and Drew and her friends having been captured by the creators, everything seems hopeless. But when a group of flawed androids rescue them, Drew is suddenly thrown into the middle of saving the world again.

Drew buries herself in the elaborate planning and scheming, as well as vigorously trying to bring Michael's memory back. But as Drew loses sight of what she cares about and her world seems like it's being ripped in two, choices are needing to be made and Drew discovers many of the people she thought she knew weren't as they appeared to be.

Betrayal, sorrow, and passion drive Drew to the limit and she's forced to choose, once again, between giving in to her desires and fears, or doing what she knows is the only right thing.

Prologue

He watched her from the doorway that led into the long, white corridor. She sat in her cell studying her hands that lay in her lap, her fingers laced together. A shadow fell across her cell leaving her in semidarkness. Her long auburn hair fell across her face, as she bent her head, not even bothering to swipe it away.

Michael's brow furrowed. She was pretty. No, he shook his head. She was beautiful. But what did that mean? The word was used for so many things, and although Michael understood the definition perfectly, knew exactly what it meant … he felt nothing. It should have some significance, shouldn't it? *She* should have some significance, shouldn't she? She had called him by his name. She had said he knew her.

But he didn't.

She had said he knew both of them, her and that other girl who was in the cell a few doors down from hers. But he had no idea who she was. He tried to remember. Tried to figure out if she was right. But whenever he tried, he came up with nothing. She was probably just confused like the creators said she was. That had to be it. The creators were always right.

He went back to watching the girl in her cell. She sat there, staring down at her hands, and although it seemed like such a boring and irrelevant thing to do, Michael couldn't seem to wrench his gaze away. Something about her held him there, something grabbed him and wouldn't let go. Something inside of him screamed at him that he knew this girl … but he didn't. That was the truth. He didn't know her. So why was he watching her?

Suddenly the girl looked up, startling him. Her eyes met his, searching his face for something. Her face was even prettier than the rest of her. She had delicate features, and her eyes were blue, the color of the sky. They looked at him with some strange expression. Hope?

"Michael," she said quietly.

At the sound of his name, Michael backed away, faster than he had intended, and in a second, he was out the door. He stood out there, staring at the wall. The color of her eyes, the sound of her voice, the way she had looked at him had brought on a strange feeling. A feeling in his heart that something had once been there. It ached with hollowness. Something inside of him screamed for him to remember.

But remember what?

Chapter One

Yvonne was smiling smugly as Michael walked my way. He passed right by me despite my efforts to talk to him. He grabbed Jessica and pulled her into a cell, clanging the door behind her. She fell to the ground with a sob and stared up at Michael with a gaze filled with despair and horror at the sight of her perfected brother.

"Michael, listen to me," I tried to say. "It's Drew and your sister Jessica."

He reached out and roughly grabbed my arm, pinching the skin so hard it hurt.

"Let go!" I yanked my arm away, took a step back, and glared at him. "You know me!" I shouted. "You have to!" My voice choked at the last part. I stared into his eyes, trying to catch a glimpse of the real Michael, but all I saw was an emotionless android staring back.

He grabbed me again and nearly threw me into the cell, slamming the door behind me. I fell against the wall and slid to the ground, rubbing my arm.

"Michael, please." My voice was a whisper.

His eyes were indifferent.

I woke with a start, tears pricking at my eyes. I sat up, rubbing my forehead. I reached over to rub my arm where Michael had grabbed me in my dream. This scene had haunted me for days—Michael staring at me, completely perfected. And each time I dreamt about it, I awoke, crying.

I could hear others shifting in the cells around me—quiet movement and sometimes sobs. Most of them coming from Jessica, a few cells down from mine.

I still couldn't believe what had happened. Every time I thought about the idea of Michael, the only person I had ever loved, being turned into a mindless android and locking us up, my mind refused to believe it. It was true; so horribly true. And I didn't even want to think about what lay in store for Jessica. She was sitting in her cell waiting to be taken away and turned into a robot like her brother.

They're going to kill you. Yvonne's words rang through my mind, and I rubbed my forehead. My fate would be completely different from Michael's and Jessica's. I had already been perfected; turned into an android. But I had gained my individuality back and, according to the creators, I was now flawed; something to be discarded. They were going to kill me. I had told myself that I wouldn't let them. That I would get away with Jessica and we would be free, but after days of sitting here, and finding no way of escape, I was beginning to doubt whether or not I would make it out of here alive.

I tried to hold back the tears. Tears of hurt, anger, and frustration, but it was getting harder and harder. A single tear slid down my cheek and dripped off the edge of my jaw line.

I wanted out. I wanted out so badly. I wanted Jessica to be free and for Michael to come back to me. But all these things, I knew, were impossible.

The creators wanted a perfect world, filled with what they considered perfect people: androids. I was in their way. I was the one who opposed them and wanted things to change. I had rebelled and now I was paying the price. I was flawed and therefore needed to be eliminated.

My thoughts floated back to Yvonne. Where was she now? Probably sucking up to the creators, getting on their good side, while she planned their annihilation. Although, I realized, she was a flawed android like me, she would never let the creators know. She claimed to be smarter, and while I sat here in this cell, I wondered if that was true. Sure she was ruthless, mean, and greedy, but she had ended up on top, right? She had turned me in because of the wrongs I had done against her, mostly for her benefit with the creators, and now she had what she had always wanted: power.

I heard Jessica call my name from her cell. "Drew?" Her voice rang through the silent corridor.

"Yeah?" I replied, hoping that my voice didn't give away the fact that I had been crying.

There was a sniffle. "Um … I don't even know what I was going to say. What can I say? I mean, what can we do about this?" Her voice choked. A tear rolled down my cheek.

I desperately wanted to say something comforting, but nothing came to mind. I wanted to fix this so badly. I wanted to say something that would make everything better; that would make the problem go away, but there were no words that could do that. We sat in silence for a few moments.

"I don't know," I finally replied. It was barely a whisper, but I knew Jessica had heard it. And for me to hear it, too, seemed to tear me apart just a little bit more. Somehow, saying that out loud was admitting that there actually was a problem; a problem from which I couldn't run away.

I leaned my head back against the wall and closed my eyes. My brain hurt from trying too hard to find a solution that wasn't there. I let out a sigh.

Hours went by and even though there were no windows or clocks, I knew it had to be late. Less people wandered past the door to our hallway, and although as an android I needed no sleep, other humans in the cells around me were slowly nodding off. I remembered the last time I was here, waiting for Yvonne to let me out. Now, I had no one upon whom to hope. There was no one out there waiting to set me free. Frustration clung to me like a virus, but I couldn't let myself lose hope yet. I couldn't do that to Jessica.

I leaned against the wall, listening to the silence around me. Everyone in the cells around me had to be sleeping by now. But suddenly the door creaked open, sending a burst of light down the dark hallway. I squinted and watched as a figure approached, female, but obscured by a large hood over her head. I had no idea who she was, and it took me a few seconds to realize she was walking straight toward my cell. I opened my mouth to ask her who she was and what she was doing here, but before I could utter a sound, she slid her hands through the bars and dropped something small and metallic onto the floor beside me. I squinted up into her face, my eyes still adjusting to the lighting, but I only glimpsed a flash of blue eyes before she turned and hurried away. I stood, ready to call after her, but she was already gone.

I stared down at the ground and kneeled, feeling around for the object she dropped. As my fingers brushed the small metallic item and I brought it closer to my face, my heart nearly stopped. I gripped it tighter into my fist and stared down the corridor where the woman had vanished.

A key.

Chapter Two

I stared down at the key in shock, every muscle frozen. Who had she been? My first thought was Yvonne. She had access to the keys, to the cells, to the whole Institution. But it couldn't have been her. She'd turned in Michael, captured Jessica and I. And when I had looked up into the face of the woman who dropped the key I had seen blue eyes, not Yvonne's black ones.

But before I could think any further or come up with a plan, the door opened once again, and the corridor flooded with light. I squinted and turned my head away, stuffing the key into my pocket. The footsteps walked down the aisle and I waited … wondering. It took me a few minutes to realize that there was more than just one person, and in fact, there were multiple people.

At first, I had thought it was the creators, or some androids, but when once my eyes had adjusted to the light, I looked up and couldn't believe what I saw.

Beatrix was smiling down at me as she calmly unlocked the door to my cell. My mind flashed back to the day when I had met her at a café and how she had explained to me her association with the flawed, a group of rebel androids.

"What…?" I barely managed to say.

She shook her head and put her finger to her lips. I scrambled to my feet, and hurried out of the cell, noticing the half-dozen others who had come along with Beatrix. I glanced down the hallway and saw Jessica's cell door being unlocked.

Jessica ran over to me, giving me a confused and frightened look.

She looked relieved, though, once she saw Beatrix. Beatrix beckoned for us to follow as she started toward the door at the end of the hallway.

"Wait." Jessica reached out to touch Beatrix's arm. "We can't go without Michael," she whispered, her eyes fearful.

Beatrix's brow furrowed, and her eyes glanced to mine and then back to Jessica's. "But isn't he…?"

"He's been perfected," I whispered hesitantly, "but we can't leave him."

Jessica was staring at Beatrix with an expression mixed with stubbornness and pleading.

Beatrix glanced at us and then at her partners. She looked at me for a long moment, opened her mouth, shut it again, and finally uttered, "Okay." She sighed. "Where is he?"

I thought for a moment. He would probably be housed where all the androids had been when I had lived here. I told her so, and we started down the hallway as quietly as we could. Beatrix tapped Jessica's arm. "Go with them while we get Michael," she whispered.

Jessica looked at me briefly and then she and a few others disappeared into the shadows. Beatrix, three of her companions, and I walked on down the hallway. I gave them a quick description of where to go, and we were soon jogging along. We hit twists and turns in the hallways, and soon we were in the corridor where the androids were housed. I prayed that there wouldn't be many around as we ventured in. I leaned over to voice my concerns to Beatrix when I saw her pull a gun from beneath her large coat. My eyes widened, and I looked at her. "Where…?" I started.

She held up a finger. "I'm not going to shoot anyone; it's just to scare them."

I shrugged, still a little surprised, and started down the hallway. I peered into one of the rooms, found it empty, and went on to the next. I knew that a lot of the androids spent their nights in the game room, as I had when I had been here. After three rooms we finally found one that contained an android.

Before I even had time to think, Beatrix had shoved the door open, aimed the pistol, and fixed the android with a steely stare.

The girl was sitting on her bed reading and dropped her book to gaze up at us. She opened her mouth as if to call out, but Beatrix gave her a warning look, and the girl closed her mouth.

"We're looking for an android named Michael," Beatrix said quietly but firmly. "He's new."

The girl looked at us, an expression of uncertainty on her face. "I…" she trailed off.

Beatrix shifted, repositioning her fingers around the trigger of the gun. "Where is he?"

The girl swallowed. "His room is number 37. Down the hall." She pointed. "I don't know if he's in there."

"If he's not in there, where would we find him?" Beatrix questioned.

The girl's brow furrowed, and she shrugged. "I really don't know. I don't know him that well. He might be in the game room." She was talking quickly, her eyes meeting each of ours. "You're flawed," she stated so calmly it sent shivers down my spine.

Beatrix ignored her. "Go," she said to one of the androids that had come with her. "See if he's in there."

The android turned and walked down the hall, and I quickly followed him. We scanned the numbers on the doors, ducking beneath the windows, and finally found number 37. I peered in and felt my heart skip a beat when I saw Michael sitting on his bed, looking up at the ceiling.

Suddenly everything came flooding back to me. How life had been at the Institution; how I had spent many boring hours doing exactly what he was doing now; looking for shapes in the drywall ceiling.

I saw this android pull out a gun as well, and I cringed at the thought of a gun being pointed at Michael. But I stood aside as he opened the door and aimed at Michael, sending my heart racing. Michael sprang to his feet and glared once he saw there was no way to stop us.

"Be absolutely quiet, or I'll shoot you," the android boy said to Michael and it sounded like he meant it. "You need to come with us, quietly," he explained.

I felt the presence of someone coming up behind me and turned to see the other android that had come along with Beatrix.

"What if I say no?" Michael asked evenly, and my heart ached at the sound of his voice saying those words.

"Then I'll shoot you."

I took in a quick breath and restrained myself from doing anything stupid. *He wouldn't kill Michael, he wouldn't kill Michael*, I kept telling myself.

There was a long pause before Michael cautiously stepped forward, glowering at the boy who held the gun.

"Stay low, below the windows," he instructed. "And be absolutely quiet. If you make any noise, stand up, or try to get away, I'll shoot you on the spot."

Michael went first, and we all crept slowly down the long corridor. Michael kept sending up frequent glances over his shoulder, and the boy kept his gun aimed at him the whole time.

When we finally reached the end of the hallway where Beatrix was still standing, watching the girl, she glanced at him and I could see relief in her eyes. We stood up next to her, the boy watching Michael while Beatrix walked into the girl's room.

"Into the bathroom," she said. The girl got up and quickly followed her orders. Beatrix closed the door behind her and turned to me. "Take Michael and get out. There's a car outside, the other androids will take you there. I'll be out in a minute."

I grabbed her arm. "You're not going to shoot her, are you?"

Beatrix shook her head. "No way, I wouldn't really shoot anyone." She said it so softly I wasn't sure I had even heard it.

I gave her one last glance and then left the room. We shuffled down the hallway, trying to be silent but run at the same time. I followed the androids and found that they had broken through a window and disabled the security cameras to get in. We crawled through the window and were soon in the parking lot sprinting toward Beatrix's van. We all climbed in, and minutes later, we saw Beatrix emerge through the broken window.

She hopped in the back seat, and the android at the wheel pulled away. Beatrix leaned her head against the headrest. Jessica smiled at me from the seats behind us, and I couldn't help but smile back, knowing that we were finally free. A wave of giddiness swept over me, and I restrained a laugh.

I couldn't help but notice that Beatrix's break-ins seemed much more successful than mine had ever been.

I looked past Michael, who was situated in the middle of Beatrix and me. "What did you do?" I asked her.

She gave a small laugh. "Shut the door and told her that if she opened it, I would shoot." She shrugged. "Then I walked away as quietly as I could and ran to the van."

I laughed too. "That was what you came up with?"

She shrugged. "The best I could do under such short notice."

"So where are we going?"

"Oh." Beatrix sat up. "That reminds me." She reached into her pocket and pulled out a large metal cube. I stared at it.

"What *is* that?" I asked her.

"Magnet," she replied, reaching for Michael's wrist. He instinctively pulled away but after the android with the gun gave him a threatening look, he surrendered his arm.

Beatrix held the magnet over his wrist for about ten seconds, and I watched her in awe. "What does that do?" I asked.

"Deactivates the tracking device by removing all the stored data." She put the magnet back in her pocket and looked at me. "Wouldn't want the creators coming after us."

"What?" Michael asked, his eyes widening. They slowly narrowed to a defiant stare.

I tried to ignore him. "So where exactly are we going?" I asked. I knew from what Beatrix had told me the last time we had met that all the flawed androids lived together, but I didn't know where. I guessed that it had to be somewhere pretty isolated, since the androids who gained their personality back were hunted and killed for their imperfections.

"It's hard to explain, but we'll be there in about thirty minutes or so," she told me.

I nodded then suddenly remembered the key in my pocket and my eyes widened. I reached in and pulled it out. "Beatrix?" I asked and she turned to me. "Did you send me this key?" I asked slowly, realizing that the timelines didn't exactly add up. Why would she send a key and then come herself only minutes later?

She leaned over and took it from me, turning it over a few times. She slowly shook her head. "No. Where did you get this?"

"Someone dropped it into my cell right before you came," I

answered.

She frowned.

"It's for the cells. I recognize it from when we've used them before."

"But who else would help you out?" Beatrix asked.

I shrugged, more unnerved now than I had been before. If the flawed hadn't sent me the key, who had?

I leaned back against the seat and stared out the window. I almost leaned my head against Michael's shoulder but then I caught myself and remembered that I could no longer do that. Part of me was overly relieved that we were finally free, but the other part was still upset about Michael. I sneaked a glance at him beside me and saw him sitting there looking uncomfortable. I desperately wanted to explain everything to him, and I desperately wanted him to understand, to remember. I thought about all the times he had looked at me with those dark brown eyes sparkling and his mouth turning upward into a smile. Those memories hurt to remember when I looked at the Michael he was now. I didn't understand how he could have forgotten me, and then I wondered how I had been when I had first been changed. What had I been like? Who had *I* forgotten?

"Drew!" I heard Beatrix call my name, yanking me out of my daydreams, and I turned just in time to see Michael lunging at my door, which I saw, too late, was unlocked. I reached out to block his way, but it did no good. He pushed right through me, threw the door open and before I knew it, he had jumped out, pushing me along with him as we flew toward the hard pavement.

Chapter Three

I tried to remember; in the split second of time when we were falling, how fast the car had been going when Michael had ungraciously thrown both of us out. I remembered the speed of the trees zipping past the windows and guessed, with some help from the highway location, that we had been going pretty fast.

My prediction rang true when we hit the pavement alarmingly hard and started rolling. I hadn't had time to untangle myself from Michael after he had shoved us out, so we went spinning together across the road. We came to a stop in the ditch along the highway and then I felt the full extent of pain from hitting the pavement. My shoulder throbbed as if something had broken, and my leg stung as if it had been scraped. I had never had this much pain so evenly dispersed across my whole body.

Just then, I realized that Michael wasn't Michael anymore and that he would most likely jump up and start running anytime now. I reached out and grabbed his wrist in a firm hold, and he looked over at me.

"You think that's going to stop me?" he spat, sitting up.

I sat up too and grabbed his other wrist. "Michael, listen," I said, knowing that he was probably as strong as I was, or stronger, so physical force wasn't going to be a major factor in keeping him there. My shoulder screamed in protest and I winced, but tried to ignore it. "You have to know who I am," I said slowly. "Please." I looked into his eyes, looking for a sign of recognition but found nothing.

"Let go of me, or I'll break your neck," he snarled, and I was taken aback by his words. And his tone. So calmly robotic.

Tears sprang to the corners of my eyes, but I angrily blinked them away. "You wouldn't," I said, but I wasn't convinced.

He yanked his arms away, but I held on firmly. That was when he lunged for my throat. I tried to hold back his arms, but he had momentum on his side. I felt his fingers slide around my neck, this time, not brushing hair away so he could kiss me, but to suffocate and break it. I panicked, realizing this was one of the first times anyone had beaten me with physical force. I shoved at him, but I couldn't stop the flow of thoughts screaming at me. *This is Michael, this is Michael.*

"Michael," I tried saying. "You don't want to do this." My shoulder seared with pain as I fell hard against the ground, and my throat was starting to ache.

"You are flawed," he said evenly, and the lack of emotion in his eyes terrified me. My vision was starting to get blurry, and his fingers were clasping tighter and tighter around my neck. "Michael!" I tried to scream.

That was when I heard noise and shouts and suddenly Michael's hands had unclasped and I was crouching, bent over, gasping for air. When I looked up, I saw three of the androids had grabbed Michael and were holding him firmly a few feet away from me.

I refused to let myself look up into Michael's eyes. I refused to let myself be hurt more than I already was. The van was parked about twenty feet away, and Jessica was standing half way between it and us, staring at Michael in shock and horror. I could see tears in her eyes as she stared at her brother accusingly.

Beatrix leaned over to help me up, and I flinched when my shoulder throbbed. We headed back to the car, the other androids pulling Michael along. We passed Jessica on the way, and she stared up at Michael with a look of disgust, her eyes staring at him reproachfully.

"How could you do that?" she whispered to him. "You *loved* her." Her voice was hard and filled with hurt. I couldn't help but wince at the past tense used in the word love.

For a second, I saw a ghost of confusion flicker across Michael's face, but soon it was gone, and I wondered if it had ever been there at all. We piled into the van once again, only this time Michael was sitting between the two male androids with pistols.

I sat in the seats behind him next to Jessica and leaned my head against the window. My heart was still racing and so was my mind. Had Michael really just tried to kill me? The thought sent my mind into a whirlwind. Michael would never try to kill me. Or at least the old Michael wouldn't. He had risked his life for me. I held back the lump in my throat and the tears that came to my eyes and busied myself with watching the scenery pass by the window.

Half an hour seemed to fly by, and soon we were pulling onto a small dirt road which led to an encampment hidden in the woods. I looked around in awe at the various tents and equipment lying around. There were two buildings, the size of average homes, and around them about twenty tents were clustered. People were milling around, and I was surprised to learn that there were so many flawed androids.

The van came to a stop next to four others parked outside the building. We all hopped out, Michael accompanied and held on to by two of the androids.

Beatrix glanced at Michael and the androids that were holding him. Then she looked back to me. She pursed her lips. "Drew, Michael will need to be held in an area where he can't get away. In taking him here, we can't risk letting him get away and telling the creators where we are." She was watching me cautiously.

I looked at her. "Where?"

She looked uncomfortable. "There's a basement inside one of the houses, and since we've been here, we've created android-proof cells."

I started to open my mouth but Beatrix cut me off.

"He'll be comfortable with a bed and chairs and things he wants, but Drew, you have to understand I can't risk the lives of all these people … just for Michael."

I looked at her for a long moment before admitting to myself that she was right. This was no longer the nice, reasonable Michael he had once been. This was the raging, perfected Michael who had, only thirty minutes ago, tried to strangle me. "Okay," I said quietly.

"Thank you," Beatrix said and mumbled something to the other androids, who then started to take Michael away.

Jessica walked up to stand beside me, but no words were said.

"Guys," Beatrix said in a lighter tone, a smile on her face. "I want you to meet some of the people here."

I smiled back, and Jessica and I followed her across the large clearing to the massive array of tents. She lifted the corner of one and ducked inside. We followed.

"Cassandra," I heard Beatrix call. Once we were inside, I saw a tall blonde girl standing up from a chair by the table where she had apparently been working on something. Her hair was long, and she had bangs which she hastily brushed out of her eyes. "Cass, this is Drew and Jessica," she said, pointing to each of us. "Guys, this is Cassandra."

She smiled at us, her light blue eyes sparkling. "Nice to meet you guys," she said.

"I had no idea there were so many of us," I told her. "It's a big relief to find you all," I told her truthfully.

Cassandra laughed and her nose crinkled as she did so. "Yeah, there *are* quite a few of us." She brushed her bangs out of her eyes again, then grabbed an elastic band and pulled back the longer pieces into a ponytail.

"Cassandra is the head of all the techie stuff," Beatrix explained with a laugh. "She's the one who came up with the magnet trick."

I looked around the room and saw it was littered with pieces of … well, anything. I had no idea what most of those things were. They looked like disassembled parts of radios or TVs. Cassandra had been working on some pile of scraps when we had come in, splayed out on the table where she had been sitting.

"Working on a way to duplicate this heater. Winter's coming, and we need a *ton* of them. And they are so expensive," she said knowingly.

"So far she's made three," Beatrix said with a smile.

Just then, someone entered the room, and Beatrix turned to greet them. "Marian!" she exclaimed. "You gotta meet Drew and Jessica."

I stiffened when I heard the name, even before I saw her face. I didn't want to turn around. I didn't want to face her, but I did anyway. When I looked at her, she seemed the same. The same long brown hair and soft brown eyes.

Her dark eyebrows knitted together when she saw me and she blinked. "Drew," she stated.

I waited, breathless. She hated me. She had to hate me. After what I had done to her, I couldn't blame her. I wanted to squeeze my eyes shut and forget, but the memories came flooding back. Back to the time when

I had wanted nothing more than to be the perfect android. When I would do anything for the creators. Like capture poor Marian, the flawed runaway, and drag her back to the Institution.

She stared at me for a long moment and then her expression softened. "I'm glad you're here," she finally said.

I blinked, surprised. She was glad? After what had happened between us?

She must have noticed my surprise because she laughed slightly. "I'm glad you're here because that means you must be flawed. You're not a *mindless* android anymore." It sounded like it should have been an insult but by her tone of voice and the expression on her face, I knew it hadn't been intended that way.

I smiled back, relieved. "I'm sorry," I started.

She held up her hand. "Don't. You don't need to be."

I smiled. I didn't need to say anything else.

Beatrix smiled a puzzled smile beside us. "Well," she said, "you guys want to see where you're going to be sleeping?"

Jessica shrugged. "Sure."

We followed Beatrix out of the tent. "I hope you guys don't mind, but you'll be sleeping in a tent," she told us with an apologetic smile.

"Oh no, that's totally fine," I reassured her. After days spent in a cold, hard cell, a tent would be more than welcome.

"At least you guys will have it to yourselves," she added. We walked across the clearing to the cluster of tents and weaved our way around them.

"Oh, by the way, Drew, I assumed you'd need rest after being at the Institution, but there's a recreation room in the first building where all the androids usually hang out at night," she explained.

"Hey, Bee!" a voice called, and we turned to see a tall blond boy jogging our way. He glanced briefly at Jessica and smiled. "Bee, who're your friends?" he asked, not taking his eyes off Jessica.

She smiled shyly back and gave me a funny look. I tried to hide my smile.

Beatrix grinned. "Drew and Jessica. We got them out of the Institution. They're going to be staying here."

"Cool." He smiled. "I'm Kyle."

"Nice to meet you," Jessica said.

"Yeah," I echoed.

"I'm just showing them their tent," Beatrix explained, beckoning for us to keep walking. We shuffled after her, noticing Kyle following as well.

"So you barely missed getting perfected?" he asked Jessica, and she nodded.

"Close call. They're getting just about everyone now," he said, and I noticed that he, once, had been perfected.

"What about you?" he asked, looking over at me.

I gave a small humorless laugh. "*Long* story," I said with a shake of my head.

He gave a knowing sigh. "Yeah, I know what you mean. The creators pretty much screw everything up. None of our lives are simple anymore." He said it lightheartedly, but there was animosity hidden in his words. We were quiet as we walked on.

I noticed as we passed tent after tent and I saw people roaming around, that most of them were teenagers, like us. I saw basically no adults; in fact, the oldest people I had seen seemed to be about nineteen or twenty. I asked Beatrix about this, and she shrugged. "Teenagers were always their first target," she reminded me. "Easier to control." The thought that the only clear thinking people around seemed to be children scared me a little.

Beatrix soon came to a small tent, opening it up for us and ushering us inside. It was tall enough for us to stand, and inside sat two cots on opposite walls. There were tons of blankets piled on each bed and a pillow for each of us. Even though it was small and impersonal, I was giddy with the relief of how much better it was to be out and away from the Institution.

"It gets pretty cold at night, so you're gonna want all those blankets," Beatrix told us.

"Thanks," I replied. "And thanks again for getting us out of there." The statement sounded lame compared to my overflowing gratitude toward the flawed, but Beatrix seemed to understand because she smiled knowingly.

"No problem."

Flawed

* * * *

Later, when Jessica and I had gone to bed, I lay awake, staring up at the tent's roof, watching the light from the stars twinkle through the fabric. I was exhausted and I knew my body needed to recharge, but somehow I couldn't fall asleep. I had been held at the Institution where I had not slept once, been stressed beyond belief, and was almost strangled recently by the boy I loved. My body and mind were completely drained. My eyelids were beginning to droop, but my brain just wouldn't turn off.

The image of Michael, determined, grabbing my throat and glaring at me, would not leave my mind. It played over and over again, and each time another tear trickled out of my squeezed-shut eyelids.

I wanted this problem to go away. I wanted Michael back. I wanted someone to hold me and tell me everything was going to be okay. To look at me in a way that let me know that I was different from everyone else; that I was special; that I was Drew, and that it was okay to be just Drew.

I felt empty. And devastated.

Alone.

Chapter Four

"I brought you some food," I said, my voice echoing throughout the quiet room. I slid the tray through the slit in the door and watched Michael stare at it, unmoving.

"And why would I want this?" he asked.

I frowned. "I know you don't *need* it, I just thought you might *like* it." I peered through the window on the door to look at him. He stared up at me from his seat on the cot.

"Why are you here?" he said.

I tried not to wince. "Because..." My thoughts trailed off. Why *was* I here? To get Michael to remember me? When I thought the words to myself I realized how foolish they sounded. "I don't know." I finally replied.

"Well if you're here to try to get me to side with all you *flawed*, you can just forget it," he snapped. He said the word 'flawed' like it tasted bad on his tongue.

"And what's wrong with us *flawed*?" I snapped back, suddenly angry.

Michael stood up and slowly walked over to the window. "It's self-explanatory," he said. "Flawed: imperfect or defective, having a problem or flaw," he stated, as if a dictionary were right in front of him. He shook his head with an almost smirk. "You take pride in being a broken, lesser version of the perfected. But you can never compare."

I glowered at him, my heart sinking even more than it already had. "There was once a time when you despised everything that had to do with the perfected. When you believed in individuality," I told him.

He snorted as if the thought of him believing such a thing was absolutely preposterous. "I must have been stupid then, because now I know better," he said simply.

I stared into his eyes for a moment, just looking, and then I turned and left the room.

I felt a lump in my throat and held back the rush of tears that came to my eyes. I walked across the large clearing, feeling the biting cold nipping at my bare arms. I looked up and just now noticed that the leaves were starting to change color. I stopped and stared for a moment. It seemed strange that the whole world was being overtaken, lives were being broken, and being ripped apart. And although everything seemed to be rushing by at lightning speed, the leaves still seemed to find time to change their color and go on with life even as everything around them was falling apart.

I sighed and kept walking, heading for the tent where I knew Beatrix would probably be.

Sure enough, she was in the tent with Cassandra, talking about something Cassandra had recently made. She looked up when I walked in. "Hey, Drew," she said with a smile.

"Hi," I said quietly, coming to sit next to them.

Her eyebrows knitted together in concern. "Talking to Michael, I presume," she said.

I nodded, not even surprised that she had guessed right.

She reached out and gently touched my arm. "Drew, believe me, we've tried. Those other perfected androids down there had gone through countless tests and talks and we've never gotten through to them," she told me. "We're working on finding a way to fix it, but so far all we've come up with is that usually it just happens, like in cases like ours."

I nodded, looking at the ground. "I hate them," I said quietly. I could tell by the silence that neither Beatrix nor Cassandra knew what to say. "I'm tired of them ruining my life."

There was a pause.

"We all are, Drew," Cassandra said, her voice edged with sympathy. "We all are."

Chapter Five

The next day, I talked to Michael again. He glared at me for awhile, said rude things, glowered some more, and finally resulted to sulking in the corner of his cell, although it was more of an android sulking than a human one. He sat motionless, expressionless, as if made of stone. After about half an hour of trying to talk, I got up and left. I wanted Michael back, but wanting just hurt, so I tried not to.

When I went in search of Jessica, I found her sitting outside on a small bench, accompanied by none other than Kyle, who seemed thrilled to be sitting and talking with her. I watched them for a moment, and I felt an ache materialize in my chest. I wasn't sure right away what the feeling was, and I didn't want to spend time trying to identify it, so I merely walked away.

Did Jessica like Kyle? I had known from day one that Kyle liked Jessica; there was no mistaking the way his eyes lit up when he saw her and how he seemed to follow her around everywhere. But did Jessica like him back? I snuck one last glance back in their direction just in time to see Jessica laughing about something that appeared to be extremely hilarious. It sure looked like she did. I couldn't help but notice that small stinging sensation in the pit of my stomach. What was that? Jealousy? I shook my head and kept walking. *I'm not ready to face that right now,* I told myself.

I found Beatrix in the main building sitting with Cassandra and Marian. "Hi," I said with a smile and sat down next to them at the table. Marian was dealing out cards of some kind.

"You wanna play?" she asked when I sat down. "You're just in time. We're starting a new game."

I smiled. "Sure. What is it?"

"Slapjack," Cassandra replied. "It's super fun; basically just slap your hand down on the pile when you see a Jack. The person with the most cards at the end wins."

I laughed. "Okay." When the cards were evenly divided we started blindly placing cards face up in the center of the table. Once the game got going it was surprisingly entertaining. A rush of adrenaline pumped through my veins at the sight of a Jack as we all aimed for the pile. It usually ended with a round of giggling and mock anger. Once the game was over and Cassandra thoroughly rubbed in the fact that she, as usual, won the game, we all settled back in our seats and started talking.

"So … do you have any idea how we could bring back the people who are perfected?" I couldn't help but ask. I had asked this quite often, but I needed to know if any changes had occurred.

"We're trying our best," Cassandra answered truthfully. "We're experimenting with the idea of a medicine or computer programming. You see, we're not even sure how the creators did this in the first place. That's the first step."

I nodded in understanding. It made sense. How were you supposed to get rid of something if you didn't know how it came about in the first place?

* * * *

"You know Kyle right?" Jessica asked me, her elbows propped up on the table, watching me from her seat. We were sitting in the main room in the building where most of the androids came to play games or just chat. There was a small table in the corner that Jessica and I were currently occupying.

I nodded. "Yeah, the guy who came and greeted us."

She nodded with a smile. "Well, I think he likes me." Her smile was wide, and her eyes sparkled.

I tried to feign excitement but at the same time I was surprised I had to fake it. Why wasn't I genuinely happy for Jessica? What was wrong with me? "That's great, Jessica," I said with a smile.

She giggled a little. "He's so nice. And he's really cute." She laughed again.

I nodded in agreement. "Yes, he's pretty cute," I teased her. "You guys look really good together. I saw you sitting on the bench the other day."

She looked at me in surprise. "You really think so? Oh, I'm so glad, I like him a lot."

I laughed. "I can tell."

Someone entered the room just then and made a beeline to where Beatrix was sitting, curled up in a chair reading a book. I glanced at him for a second and then turned back to Jessica. "So when did you decide you liked him?" I asked her.

She made a thoughtful look. "Hmmm..." she said. "Probably a few days after we got here." She laughed again. "He was just so nice to me, and he's so funny..." Her voice suddenly became unimportant as I heard a word from across the room. They said it in a hushed tone, but that word would turn my head anywhere.

"...Yvonne..." I swiveled around in my chair to see Beatrix and the boy who had come in talking together.

"Drew, are you okay?" Jessica asked me.

I nodded. "Yeah, I'll be right back." I stood up from my chair and walked across the room. Beatrix saw me and beckoned me closer. "Daniel just gave me some news," she told me. "And I think you already know that." She gave a halfhearted smile. "Yvonne's been appointed co-leader at the Institution," she told me frankly. "You knew her, didn't you?" she asked me.

I nodded. I took a step back. Somehow this news wasn't surprising to me. I knew Yvonne would get there; the only question had been when. But the news still came as a shock, a shock that now the creators were even more unpredictable, then they already had been. With Yvonne in power—well, I didn't want to think about the consequences of that. I knew they weren't good.

"Drew?" I heard Jessica's voice call from across the room, and with one last glance at Beatrix, I headed her way. "Is everything alright?" she asked me.

I shrugged. "Beatrix just told me that Yvonne has been appointed co-leader at the Institution," I replied.

Jessica's eyes widened. "Really?" she asked.

I nodded. "I can't say I'm surprised though," I said.

Jessica nodded in understanding. "Yeah, I know what you mean." We were quiet for a moment. "It's so weird, just the two of us," she barely whispered it, but I didn't need to hear it again to know what she meant.

It had always been the three of us: Jessica, Michael and I who would discuss these things. We were always together. We always had each other's backs. And now, he was gone.

I watched as a tear escaped out of the corner of Jessica's eye, though she tried to blink it away. "I miss him," she said softly.

I nodded, unable to say anything in fear that I might break down and cry. "We'll get him back," I was finally able to say. "I know we will. Eventually," I said it with meaning, but I wasn't sure who I was trying harder to convince, Jessica or myself.

She nodded with a small smile. "Yeah. We gotta keep up our faith." She smiled a little more.

I smiled halfheartedly back.

Jessica's face suddenly turned into a grin, and I didn't need to turn around to see what had caused it. I already knew. Kyle had entered the room.

Chapter Six

I lay on my cot in the tent, staring up at the moonlight penetrating the fabric. It was such a funny light. Eerie and on the edge of creepy, but beautiful at the same time.

Images from the day flitted through my mind. Kyle coming in to get Jessica; her musical laugh caused by some goofy joke of his. Beatrix raising her eyebrows and nudging me as they walked out. My forced laugh as we discussed how cute a couple they could be. The image of Kyle's lips against Jessica's when I saw them later outside.

I closed my eyes, trying to hold in the rush of tears. I felt one escape and go sliding down my cheek and onto my neck. The feeling of it moving across my skin sent a shudder through my body.

Jessica sighed in her sleep across the tent, and I glanced over. Her face was shadowed, and I looked away. Why did it hurt so much to see Jessica and Kyle together? The question was unanswerable, but I wondered it anyway.

My mind wandered to Michael. I remembered the times he had kissed me. The way nothing in the world seemed to matter except for the sensation of kissing him. The way he used to look at me, as if I was the only person in the world.

Something inside my chest started to ache, and I stopped the flow of memories. I had been over them dozens of times, trying to relive the moments that were slowly slipping out of my grasp. I missed Michael. I missed him too much.

* * * *

I sat alone, once again, in the game room, looking out the window as Jessica and Kyle walked hand in hand. Why I was doing this to myself, I didn't know. Torturing myself over Jessica's happiness. It was selfish and I knew it. I needed to stop. A voice startled me, and I turned around to see Beatrix standing in the doorway.

"Drew, you wanna come with me to town?" she asked. "We're low on medicine and first aid supplies. You know, aspirin, bandages, antiseptic…"

I shrugged and smiled. "Sure." We left the building and headed for one of the cars parked in the clearing. Beatrix pointed to a silver truck, and I jumped in the passenger seat. She turned the key and pulled out onto the long dirt path leading away from the camp. I had a feeling she had only asked me to come along to help brighten my mood.

"Cameron told me this morning we needed more supplies," Beatrix told me as we drove. "He's the head of all the medical stuff," she reminded me.

I nodded. "Are injuries common?"

She shrugged. "Sometimes. We just always want to be prepared. When we went to get you, Jessica, and Michael, we had some minor injuries, and we could have conceivably gotten way worse. We always like to have more than we need, just in case," she explained.

I nodded.

We spent the rest of the car ride listening to music on the radio, Beatrix often singing along to songs she knew. When we finally pulled up to the grocery store, we both hopped out and headed inside.

"So how long have you been flawed?" I asked Beatrix quietly as we were studying the medicine aisle.

"A few months or so," she said. "It's not like it hit me all of a sudden. It was a slow process," she admitted. "The flawed found me, and I escaped with them." She turned to me and shrugged. "Pretty simple." She reached for a bottle of aspirin.

"How about the others?" I asked.

"Cassandra's been there for quite awhile. At least that's what I've heard," Beatrix told me. "Marian just got here about a month ago. All of us are fairly new."

I nodded.

Beatrix turned to me. "Hey, why don't you keep watch outside while I check out?" she asked.

I nodded, turned, and headed for the door. It was windy outside, and I pulled my sweater tighter around me as I looked around at the street and the buildings surrounding me.

Nothing looked out of the ordinary. No one seemed to be watching or following us. I tried to let myself relax, but I knew I would never be fully comfortable again out in the open. I rubbed my hands together to keep warm, hoping Beatrix would hurry up.

For a second I thought of the Institution. I wondered if all the creators had been perfected by now. Probably. Why not? Why not become perfect like their subjects? I just wondered why they hadn't tried it out on themselves first, before creating us.

A flash of something tall and dark caught my eye from across the street, and I looked up

My heart stopped. My breath caught in my throat, and I stared into the dark eyes of the last thing I ever wanted to see.

Yvonne stopped walking and was staring at me; her eyes were expressionless. I stared back; frozen, unable to do anything else but stand there and watch her. I couldn't think straight. The only words that swiveled through my mind were ones I didn't want to hear. *Co-leader of the Institution.* The phrase repeated itself over and over again. She was so close. So close to being in complete and utter control. Why stop now? Why pass up the perfect opportunity to make the creators love her even more than they already did? I shook my head and shut my eyes for a brief moment, as if to say, *Okay Yvonne, you win.* What more could I lose?

It was over.

She kept staring at me, her eyes boring into mine, and it finally hit me. She was thinking. Rarely did Yvonne ever think. She always acted impulsively. Whatever seemed the best thing at the time, she did it. I widened my eyes in shock. She was deciding whether or not she wanted to save my life or end it.

She tilted her head and smiled at me. Her eyes seemed to suggest she was laughing at me. But not in a cruel way, just in *her* way. She shook her head and turned to leave, but looked back one last time. She raised her eyebrows as if in farewell, and then turned and headed down the street.

In shock, I watched her go until she was out of sight, and then I let a breath of relief escape me. For a moment, I wondered if it had ever happened – if I had really just seen her. And she'd done … nothing.

Yvonne had chosen me over power. She had let me go.

Chapter Seven

I pulled the bottle of aspirin out of the bag, ready to be put on the shelf in the bathroom. The lights weren't on, so I leaned closer to the window to read the label. Two pills for the average size adult. Two pills would kill the pain.

I stared at the label for a minute. I wondered if it actually worked on androids. Well, probably, otherwise Beatrix wouldn't have gotten it. Rarely did I ever get headaches, so I'd never used a painkiller before. The hospital had probably given me some when I had been shot though, but that would have been the first.

I had heard of overdosing on pain medications, and I wondered if that applied to androids as well. After all, I had gotten shot in the back, fallen off a roof, and been fine the next day. Could pain killers really hurt me?

I shrugged and put the bottle away in its place. Nothing would kill the pain I had, anyway. I guess there was just too much of it.

Just then, Cassandra walked in, a candy cane in her mouth. "Hey Drew."

I smiled. "Hi."

She opened the cabinet and pulled out a toothbrush. She looked at it for a second, frowned, sighed, and shrugged.

I laughed. "What are you doing with that?" I asked her.

"The heater we have is being weird. It thinks it needs to be cleaned," she explained. She turned to leave the room and, I followed.

"Whose toothbrush?" I asked.

"Cameron's," she smiled mischievously. "But he won't mind."

I laughed. We walked outside and toward the tent where Cassandra kept all her heaters, computers, tools, and whatever else she happened to be working on. We passed the house where Michael was being kept, and I quickly looked away.

"You haven't gotten any closer to figuring out how to, you know, deperfect people?" I asked her tentatively.

Cassandra sighed. "A little bit." We reached the tent, and she sat down at a table where various heaters and parts lay scattered around. "All I can think of is that it's like breaking through a series of walls; everything gets clearer the more walls you break down." Cassandra pulled the back of a heater off and started scrubbing with the toothbrush. "It can come naturally like it did with you and the others. Rebellious thoughts and refusal to accept certain things can cause the walls to break, but I think those walls can also be forced to collapse, I just don't know how yet."

Walls. The idea made sense. Things did start to get clearer gradually. "But how could you force it?" I asked.

Cassandra shrugged. "That's the tough part," she said. "From what we've learned about other flaweds' experiences, it could be caused by trauma, a certain memory suddenly activated; things like that," she explained.

I had tried to activate Michael's memory many times. I told him about things he had done, things Jessica and I had done. I had even hoped that just my presence there would help him remember, but nothing had happened. I closed my eyes, aware of a sudden urge to cry.

"Thanks Cassandra," I said with a smile and turned to leave. The cold hit me hard as I left the tent, and tears pricked the corners of my eyes. This time I didn't try to stop them or brush them away. I just let one slowly trickle down my cheek.

I saw Jessica hurrying my way, a bright smile on her face, and I tried to quickly hide my tears, not wanting to dampen her mood.

"Drew, I need to tell you something about Kyle and I, so we were sitting…" she trailed off. "Drew, are you okay?" Her smile was gone, her voice edged with concern.

I shrugged. "I'm okay," I told her quietly.

She shook her head. "No you're not. You're crying."

I shrugged again. "I was just talking to Cassandra about curing the perfected."

"Michael…" Jessica said quietly.

I nodded.

Jessica's eyes widened. She covered her mouth. "Oh, I'm so sorry Drew," she said suddenly. "I've been going on and on about Kyle and me, not even realizing how much that must hurt you, with Michael." She swallowed. "Oh, Drew, I'm so sorry." Now Jessica looked near tears.

I shook my head. "No, it's not your fault. You deserve to be happy with Kyle, you don't need to stop talking about it or anything," I told her.

Jessica leaned over to hug me. I hugged her back and let one more tear escape. "You know, God will take care of all this." Jessica told me. "You just need to have faith in that."

I pulled out of her hug, and we started walking. "I don't know about that," I said quickly.

Jessica stopped and looked at me. "What?" she asked, a frown slowly seeping into her expression.

I shook my head, suddenly angry. "How do you know that God even cares about me?" I asked her, my voice coming out more accusatory than I had intended. "Why would He take Michael away from me if He cared?"

Jessica stared at me, shocked. "Drew, you don't mean that," she said slowly.

"Yeah, actually I think I do," I told her. "I pray about things, and nothing happens. I pray so hard, I think I might die. I pray over and over again, so many times…" My voice was rising. "And Michael's still in there, *a robot*," I cried. "He stares at me like I'm nothing to him! *Nothing.*" Jessica's expression looked hurt.

"God cares about you Drew. Terrible things happen, but He always has a plan."

I shook my head in frustration. "I'm not even human." I barely whispered. "So why would He care?" I turned and ran, not wanting to hear Jessica's response and not wanting to see the look of hurt that I knew was etched on her face.

Chapter Eight

I heard crying, and it took me a moment to realize that it was Jessica. It was getting louder. It had been a few days since our fight, and we hadn't really talked a whole lot since then.

I stood up. "Jessica?" I called down the hallway. I left the game room and started walking. Where was she? I heard footsteps and then a door opening. The bathroom. I followed the noise and knocked on the bathroom door. "Jessica?"

The door swung open. Jessica was leaning against the counter, grabbing a handful of tissues to wipe her eyes. She looked up when the door opened, her eyes red and puffy.

"What's wrong?" I asked her, suddenly afraid.

She sniffed and wiped a tear off her cheek. "Kyle's gone," she said quietly.

"What?" I asked, not sure what she meant.

She shook her head, starting to cry again. "He went out this morning with some of his friends." She stopped for a minute to catch her breath. "They were just getting food." She started crying again, and I took a step forward to hug her. She kept talking into my shoulder. "He was the only one who didn't make it back. The creators—I don't know how they found him, but they did." Her body shook slightly, and I hugged her tighter. "They'll kill him, Drew," she sobbed.

I closed my eyes. Yes. I knew. "Jessica, I'm so sorry," I said quietly, still hugging her. She only cried harder.

* * * *

Half an hour later, we sat at the table in the game room talking. Cassandra, Beatrix, Cameron, Jessica, and I. Jessica's eyes were still red from crying, and all the others looked upset and tired.

"We need to get him back," Jessica said for the hundredth time.

Cassandra shook her head wearily. "Jessica, we can't," she said sadly. "We can't afford to right now. They're expecting us to come back for him."

"But he'll die!" Jessica cried, her eyes starting to tear up again.

Cassandra started rubbing her forehead, looking upset. Beatrix glanced my way, and we exchanged looks.

"Kyle will have to stay put for the time being," Cameron explained. "Maybe in a few days we can get a plan together and rescue him, but not this very second."

A tear escaped Jessica's eye. "But he doesn't have that long," she said quietly. "He's flawed; he's of no use to them. They'll just get rid of him."

"They might want him alive to get information about the flawed," Beatrix said truthfully. "It means he's probably not going to be living under nice circumstances, but he'll be alive," she said.

Jessica flinched slightly, and then she closed her eyes. "I can't just not do anything," she said. "Please…"

"In a few days we'll get him," Cameron told her. "I'm sorry."

A half-sigh, half-sob escaped Jessica's throat as Cassandra, Beatrix, and Cameron got up from their seats. Beatrix walked over and placed a hand on her shoulder. "I'm sorry," she said and then they all left.

The room was quiet once the others had gone, and we just sat there for a few seconds, saying nothing.

"We'll find a way to get him back," I said quietly after a long pause. "We'll get a plan and—"

"No," Jessica interrupted me, looking up. "Don't you understand, we *can't* wait." She looked at me with her brown, pleading eyes. "Don't you remember how fast they perfected Michael? It was a few hours! And he was gone!" She was crying again. "I can't let them hurt Kyle."

I sighed. "Like Beatrix said, he's an important source of information," I explained.

"You wouldn't just sit here and do nothing if it was Michael who had been taken away," Jessica cried, her eyes boring into mine accusingly.

I stared at her for a moment. Her hands gripped the table that was varnished so brightly, her reflection shone on the wood, as if not only one Jessica, but two were staring me down.

No. I probably wouldn't have just sat around and waited for a plan. I would've wanted to go right away. I knew that running in there without a plan was too great a risk. But Jessica wasn't willing to see that. Because she was in love. I knew how that felt. The hardest part was that I understood *exactly* how she felt. I knew what it was like to lose that person. I knew all too well. I knew what it felt like to be helpless and dangling, unsure whether everything was going to turn out all right.

That's why it hurt me so much to tell her the truth. To tell her that risking the other's lives wasn't fair. To tell her the things I wish someone had told me when I was too blind to see it for myself.

"I'm sorry Jessica," I told her. "I'm sorry."

Chapter Nine

Seclusion is a funny thing. It tends to make you pay attention to details. It forces you to study the things you once took for granted. The little things. The things you pass by every day but you never really see. I had been living in the woods for about a month now, and I had noticed how many things I would just stop and watch. Such as my gaze wandering to a tiny leaf dangling precariously on a tree branch, it's every twitch, it's every vein, color, and size until it would finally flutter to the ground and disappear into the mass of others just like it. How a bird seemed something special and unique when before it was nothing, but just another bird. How a forest would seem silent at first glance, but when you looked again you saw that it was teeming with life. The little things that you needed to slow down to actually see.

I had never really been in a forest before. Not like this. I had run through them. But that didn't really count.

I looked up at the fading night sky, the stars twinkling faintly as if saying goodbye and I wondered what time it was. I had wandered out here in the early hours of the morning, and by now it must have been five or six in the morning.

A dark blue was slowly seeping into the blackness of the night, leading the way to morning. I hugged my large coat tighter around me and let out a breath of air and watched it slowly fade away.

For a second I let myself think of Michael. He would've liked it out here. He liked simple things. Little things like holding my hand and smiling. He didn't need to give me roses or presents to let me know how he felt. I already knew.

I turned my attention to the moon that was slowly sinking down toward the horizon. I didn't want to think about Michael anymore. The moon shone bright and beautiful. Perfect. *Are we supposed to be perfect like you?* I wondered. My mind wandered to the perfected and how they could be cured. My head hurt. I felt as if I had gone through every possibility and found nothing. I wanted to kick something. Anything.

I sighed instead. *Calm down, Drew.* I told myself. *Take a step back.* I thought for a moment. Simple. Make it simple. How are robots controlled? Computers? Did we have programming? I widened my eyes. Did we? Did they? The new ones? I remember Yvonne telling me how the newer androids were programmed…

Suddenly I heard noises. I turned. I saw a figure in the darkness about twenty feet ahead, and I was about to instinctively run when I heard the voice. "Drew!" Beatrix called. "Drew!"

Something hit me in the chest. A bad feeling. The anxiety in her voice.

Something was wrong.

I ran toward Beatrix through the darkness. "What's wrong?" I asked her.

She grabbed my arm and tugged me along. "It's Jessica," she said. "She's gone. She must have run away. We can't find her. We thought you had gone, too."

I stopped. "She's gone?" I echoed. To find Kyle?

Beatrix nodded, looking distressed. "Was she out here with you?" she asked, her voice hopeful.

I shook my head. "She was sleeping in the tent when I left," I said.

Beatrix let out a sigh of frustration. "She's gone to find Kyle."

"But how?" I cried. "Alone?"

Even in the dark I could see the look of sadness on Beatrix's face. "Alone," she answered. "There's nobody else missing."

No. The word swirled through my mind. She couldn't go alone. It was too dangerous. She couldn't have … but she did.

I reached out to touch Beatrix's arm. "We have to stop her," I said quietly, looking up to meet her eyes.

She frowned slightly. A sad frown. "Drew…" She started to slowly shake her head. "By now she must be there already, and you know we can't go right now."

I let out a frustrated sigh and started rubbing my forehead where a headache had suddenly appeared. "Well then, what do we do?" I asked quietly, although I already knew the answer. We wouldn't do anything. We would wait. Going in to try to save Jessica would be a suicide mission, and everybody knew that.

Beatrix was silent for a moment. "Maybe we can get her back before they … perfect her," she said quietly, a small hopeful smile on her lips.

I shook my head. No. I was tired of lying to myself. About Michael. About everything. "No," I said. "She's gone."

Chapter Ten

"Michael," I said. "Jessica, your sister, she's gone," I told him. I watched his face, which was partly obscured by shadows.

"I don't have a sister," he said impatiently.

I closed my eyes, trying to find the patience I needed. I opened my mouth to reply, but no words came. What could I say? I'd already said everything I could think of. I'd said everything I could imagine. And it wasn't enough. Instead, I just sat there, staring at my hands in my lap. I leaned back from my kneeling position to sit on the ground, feeling the cold of the cement floor seep through my jeans and into my skin. I felt like crying, but I was all cried out. There were no more tears left inside me. Just disappointment, sorrow, despair; emptiness.

I sensed Michael shifting in his cell.

"You're in pain," he said slowly.

I looked up, my eyes meeting his.

"But there's nothing wrong with you," he added. "You're not hurt, but you're hurting." His eyebrows furrowed in robotic puzzlement.

I swallowed and nodded. "Yes. I am," I replied, feeling intrigued by his sudden interest and confusion.

Michael stared at me for a moment, his eyes narrowed as if trying to decipher a strange code. "Why?" he finally asked.

Why. What a good question. Because everything that used to matter to me had somehow been torn away, pushed away, or taken away, and there was nothing left to hold on to. That was why. But how did you explain sorrow to someone who doesn't understand emotions?

"Because somebody hurt me," I told Michael quietly, thinking of

Glen and the creators; the masterminds behind this new world. Because ultimately it wasn't Michael who hurt me by forgetting, it was the creators who took away his life, his choice. My life, my choice.

"But why would they hurt you?" he asked.

I was quiet for a minute. Why *did* they hurt me? I didn't even know myself. Maybe because they were so hungry for the idea of a perfect world, so caught up in their plans for a rebirth, that they didn't even realize the people they crushed along their way.

"I don't really know," was the answer I finally settled on.

Michael made a thoughtful sound. "Were they humans?" he asked, as if he already knew the answer. *Of course they were humans, only humans could make mistakes like that,* he must have been thinking. I could see it in his eyes.

I nodded. "Yes. They were once."

Michael half-smiled in a knowing way. "Yeah. Humans are like that."

For some reason I felt like Michael had just connected with me. As if he had realized that perfected or flawed, neither of us were truly human any longer.

"Humans have no right to hurt the perfected," he started telling me. "They're insignificant and don't mean nearly as much as the perfected do." I could hear the superiority in his voice and see it in his eyes as well. He hated the humans. Just like the creators wanted him to.

What a perfect android.

"But don't worry." He turned to me as if to console me, and I was surprised by his sudden opening up toward me. "The humans aren't worth your pain." His dark eyes bore into mine with a gaze that he must have meant to be consoling, but it only worried me.

I stared at Michael for what seemed like an eternity, torn between staying there and agreeing with him or turning to leave. I desperately wanted to agree, to say that he was right, because in doing so, Michael would turn to trusting me again and more than anything, I wanted his trust. His trust was just one step closer to where we had been, and something inside of me ached with the longing for that.

But I knew he was wrong. I knew he had been brainwashed, turned into something that he wasn't. And no matter how hard I struggled against that reality, I couldn't get up the nerve to tell Michael he was right and see the sparkle in his eyes.

"No, Michael," I said sadly, not wanting to shatter these few moments of harmony, but knowing there was nothing else I could do. "They weren't just humans."

He watched me.

"They were the creators," I barely whispered. And then I turned, not wanting to see his face change from the most I had seen of Michael in weeks, back to the cold, hard android that I knew would never change.

Chapter Eleven

Marian watched me from across the room. Our eyes hadn't met yet, but I could tell she saw me. I felt her gaze resting on me. I propped my elbow up on the table and leaned my head against my hand, watching whatever happened to be passing by outside the window.

I had recently trudged into the game room, probably looking upset and dejected, which was how I felt. I couldn't go back to the tent where Jessica and I had spent a lot of our time talking the past few weeks. I couldn't go back there without Jessica.

I sighed and looked up, meeting Marian's gaze.

She smiled slightly. "Drew, you okay?" she asked tentatively.

I shrugged. Marian got up from her seat and walked over to me. She sat down across from me at the table. "You know, we've all lost people..." she said quietly. "I know what it feels like," she added sympathetically.

I nodded. I believed her. I hadn't missed the layer of sorrow hidden beneath each of the flaweds' seemingly happy personalities. I looked up. "Does it get better?" I asked with a humorless laugh, surprised I was actually asking the question.

Marian shrugged.

I looked down at my hands, which were resting on the table, feeling tears prick the corners of my eyes. I sniffed. "Even if he does come back though..." I started to say, knowing I had to tell someone. I couldn't keep this in any longer. This terrible doubt that was consuming me. "What if he doesn't remember me?" I whispered the last part.

I didn't need to look up to know that Marian was lost for words. The silence that followed assured me of that.

"But—"

I looked up to see Marian's expressions clouded with confusion. "Why wouldn't he remember you?"

I frowned slightly. "Because even though I'm flawed, I've never remembered people from my past before the Institution."

Marian watched me for a moment, her light brown eyes searching for something she couldn't find. "You never remembered anyone?" she finally asked.

I slowly shook my head. "No. Did you?"

Marian nodded. "Yeah. We all did. We remembered our homes, being taken away from them, kidnapped, our siblings, friends…"

I stared at her for a moment, unsure whether this was true. I knew some of the flawed remembered things, but did they all? "All of them?" I asked. "Are you sure?"

She nodded slowly, still staring at me with a puzzled expression. "All except you."

Suddenly I couldn't sit. I needed to get up, to move, to run. I stood up from my chair so quickly it made a screech of protest as it slid across the floor. I walked to the window and back again. "Why?" I asked Marian. "Why would everyone remember except me?" I ran my fingers through my hair and then let my hand rest at the back of my neck for a moment. "Everyone?" I asked Marian again. "You're positive?"

She nodded. "I'm pretty sure. I've never come across someone who hasn't before now."

There was a pause while I stood, staring at my hands, barely breathing as Marian watched me.

"Drew…" she said eventually. I looked up to meet her gaze. Her eyes were lined with confusion, sympathy, and … caution? She swallowed as if rethinking her phrase. "Maybe there's nothing to remember."

"Nothing to remember?" I repeated blankly.

Marian nodded. "You said you have memories of being a child at the Institution?" she asked me.

I nodded slowly, now starting to understand. "But," I started, "I was human at some point. I had to have had a mother and father; a life. I wasn't created there." The words came out more accusatory and defensive than I had intended.

"Drew," Marian replied in a soothing tone. "I'm not saying this is true, but you have to admit it's a possibility." Her eyes were lined with sympathy, but I didn't want her pity.

I shook my head. I didn't want to be defined by my life at the Institution. I didn't want that to be the only part of me. I wanted something else ... something human. "No," I said. I opened my mouth to say more but nothing came. I closed my eyes. I had fought so hard. So hard to find out what I really was. My past. And then I had fought again to reclaim the one thing that could define me as an individual; a soul. I had wanted it more than anything in the world, and even though I had found it, here I was still wrestling with the facts about what I really was; still fighting for my wish to be human. Because it seemed that no matter how hard I held onto it, it was never hard enough.

"That doesn't make you who you are," Marian told me softly, as if reading my mind. "What you do, how you act, that's what makes you who you are."

I opened my eyes and found them filled with tears. I brushed them away before they could escape.

"The Institution can change *what* you are," Marian told me, "but they can't change *who* you are." With that, Marian smiled and quietly left the room.

I stood still as her words swirled through my head. What. Who. *They are different things,* I told myself. They had changed what I was; they had changed me into something mechanical. But they hadn't changed who I was.

Who I was. The phrase seemed to stick in my mind; to slowly push its way through my thoughts. I thought about it for a moment. Who was I? I searched for an answer and my expression formed into a frown.

I didn't know who I was. And that's what scared me the most.

Chapter Twelve

I felt something grasp my hand, and I opened my eyes with a start to see Michael. Not the perfected Michael, but the old one, standing there, hovering over my bed, and looking into my eyes. I sat up, not looking away from his gaze as he pulled me out of the tent and into the cold, late autumn night.

We started running, and I suddenly realized I was laughing. He talked to me, telling me about how he'd missed me. His eyes were sparkling.

We came to a stop in a meadow; although how we got there I wasn't sure. Michael let go of my hand. I saw Jessica standing about ten feet away, and I opened my mouth to call to her when I realized that she wasn't human anymore. My words formed into something unintelligible; something closer to a scream. I turned to look at Michael, to see if he saw this as well, but then I saw that his features were no longer comforting and imperfect, but rigid as he turned into an android.

My eyes flew open, and I noticed I was sitting up in bed. I was certain that my scream hadn't only been in my sleep. I closed my eyes and started rubbing my forehead. Why had I even wanted to sleep tonight? I hadn't slept in weeks, and even though I was an android, I needed to recharge. But I should've known that sleeping would come with nightmares.

I lay back against my pillow as I watched the color of the tent change from black to a bright glow as the sun rose. Even though morning had come, I didn't get up right away. There didn't seem to be a good enough reason, so I just lay there, letting the warmth and comfort take over.

Eventually I got up and left the tent. I smoothed down my hair as I walked out into the clearing and didn't bother changing because I had gone to sleep in my clothes from yesterday, anyway.

I walked past the houses, past the cars, and down the dirt road about twenty feet. I stopped and stared at the trees around me. I wondered briefly if there even was a meadow anywhere near here. The thought brought me back to my dream, and I shook my head trying to rid myself of it.

Suddenly I saw a figure approaching in the distance, and at first, I thought it was a figment of my imagination, just like the dream had been. But as it got closer, I began to realize that it was real. I took a step backward, ready to run and warn the others, but then I noticed that the person was limping.

I started to walk slowly toward him and then I saw that the person was carrying something else. And then everything clicked into place, and my eyes widened.

Kyle and Jessica.

I started to run, calling their names and calling to the others near the tents to follow me.

I got closer, and I noticed that Kyle's expression had changed to a relieved one, knowing help was on the way. And then my gaze turned to Jessica…

I stopped running so quickly that I almost fell over. I started to shake my head.

Dreams don't come true.

But I couldn't dismiss the fact that the unconscious Jessica that lay in Kyle's arms was taller, had longer legs, longer arms, and her skin tone didn't quite match the girl I used to know.

My mouth was dry, and it seemed like I had lost the ability to speak. I finally came to my senses after a few seconds and realized that, perfected or not, Kyle needed help getting her back to the camp.

I started walking toward him. I couldn't bring myself to run, knowing that every step closer would only confirm that this awful nightmare was true.

I was the first to reach Kyle and Jessica and when I did, Kyle sank to his knees in the dirt. I helped him gently put Jessica on the ground, and I couldn't help but hold in a gasp at the sight of her. My Jessica.

She wasn't my Jessica anymore.

I looked at Kyle, taking in his bloody and disheveled appearance. "Where are you hurt?" I asked him. I heard footsteps running up behind me, and I knew others had come.

He shook his head. "Not sure…" he was breathing hard. "I … couldn't get her before she was perfected." He stared desperately into my eyes as if searching for my forgiveness.

I shook my head. "You brought her back," I told him. "Thank you."

He nodded, trying to catch his breath. "It's a miracle we got out. Jessica was struggling … she's not…" he trailed off.

Cassandra, Cameron, and a few other flawed appeared beside us, and Cameron started checking Kyle and Jessica for injuries right on the spot.

"Kyle," Cassandra said slowly. "Did you…?"

He nodded before I even knew what she was talking about. "The tracking device is disabled."

Just then I noticed Jessica stirring, and I looked down to see her eyelids flutter open. At first she just looked at us in confusion and then she seemed to understand where she was and her eyes widened. She sat up, but Kyle and Cameron were already there to stop her. She kicked and starting screaming at them.

I had to take a step back in shock. There are some things you can never prepare yourself for.

Cameron and Kyle hauled Jessica to her feet and started dragging her back to the camp. She struggled the whole way, and even when she met my gaze, she kept shouting. I didn't know why I thought I would make a difference. Deep down I knew she wouldn't remember me, but it seemed like yet another hope had been crushed when I looked into her eyes as she screamed at me.

As Cassandra and Cameron started leading the way to the house where Michael was kept, Kyle stopped short. "We can't put her in there," he protested accusingly.

Cassandra glared at him over the kicking and screaming Jessica.

"There's no other choice, Kyle," she said sternly. "And we don't have a lot of time to talk about this." She gestured to Jessica, who was trying to bite Kyle's hand.

They hurried her inside and put her in the cell next to Michael's. I couldn't help but cringe at the sight of them both locked up and glaring at me with bloodthirsty eyes. It made me think of the Institution and how we had been locked up, and suddenly I wanted so badly to let them go, but this was war—a fact that I was slowly beginning to realize.

We walked up the stairs and left the house as I listened to Jessica's shouts slowly diminish and finally disappear.

All four of us stopped outside the door and just stood there, letting the wind whip at our hair and clothing, stealing any warmth we had left.

Cameron shifted his feet in the dirt. "You know, we can't just continue keeping them here."

Kyle looked up swiftly and stared at him in angered shock.

"I mean, the perfected in general, not the individual ones that you both saved," Cameron backpedaled. He sighed. "All I'm saying is that we don't have that much room to house this many perfected, especially if they are enhancing them," he explained firmly.

"Well, I'm sorry if this is an inconvenience to you," Kyle snapped, his eyes blazing.

"Hey, we all have people we love who have been perfected," Cameron shot back. "It's just that not all of us have the luxury of keeping them in cages like pets!"

Kyle lunged for Cameron, hitting him and tackling him to the ground. Cassandra started yelling at both of them and hauled Kyle up off of Cameron, who lay glaring, wiping away the blood on his mouth.

"Enough!" Cassandra spat. "We don't need this. Neither of you do."

Cameron scrambled up from the ground, took one last glance at Kyle, shook his head, and walked away.

I watched him leave. I had never seen Kyle or Cameron act this way. They were friends. But I knew that Jessica being perfected had upset everything.

Cassandra sighed as she watched Cameron disappear into one of the tents. "So did you learn anything important while you were there?" she asked halfheartedly as if she really didn't care at the moment, but she knew she should ask anyway.

Kyle shrugged. "Not really…" he trailed off. "Oh," he added, looking up to meet my gaze. "I did hear some things about Yvonne," he said slowly.

My brow furrowed. That name always brought bad memories.

"Apparently they found out about her plans of … well, whatever her plans had always been," he said with a shrug, and I thought about Yvonne's constant ranting about her want for complete power. "Well, the creators found out that she was planning against them." My eyes widened. Yvonne would never be that careless. Kyle shifted as if not sure how to convey his next message. "They said they were going to kill her," he said simply.

I stood there for a moment, staring at him in shock, unmoving, unspeaking. "Kill her?" I echoed in disbelief. Yvonne, killed by the creators? She was too smart for that. She was way too smart for that. Too smart to even be caught. But yet she had.

Kyle shifted uncomfortably. "You guys weren't friends, were you?" he asked slowly.

I opened my mouth and then helplessly shrugged my shoulders. "It's complicated," I finally told him, but it came out as a whisper.

Suddenly my mind was racing, coming up with ideas on how Yvonne could escape. On how she would dodge her imminent death. On how I would help her, because even though Yvonne had stabbed me in the back countless times, she had let me go in the street when I had seen her weeks ago. And no matter how hard I tried to forget it, I couldn't shake the memories of being a kid with her; of being friends.

"When…?" was all I could manage to utter.

Kyle's expression melted into a frown. "Um, by now, Drew." He threw his hands upward in defeat. "I'm sorry, Drew, I didn't know you guys were close." He closed his eyes. "She's already dead."

Chapter Thirteen

I remember Kyle asking me if I was okay, but I don't remember answering. All I could think about was the fact that Yvonne was dead. Everything inside of me told me that I knew Yvonne and that it was impossible for her to be dead. The words that had come out of Kyle's lips told me otherwise, and I knew Kyle wouldn't lie. Yvonne dead. Yvonne dead. Yvonne couldn't be dead. But she was.

I didn't know what I felt. Shock, sorrow, loss? None seemed to quite fit. I was upset in a way I had never known before. I wasn't upset like I had been when Michael and Jessica had been perfected, feeling the loss of a friend, of someone you love. My feelings went much deeper than that. To a part of me I couldn't explain, a part of me I hadn't explored. I felt empty, confused, shocked, and sad all in one rush of emotion, and I didn't know what it meant.

Was I crying? I blinked before the tears escaped. Had I really loved Yvonne? Deep down, had I really forgiven her for everything she'd done and continued to love her, to want to love her, to want her to change? I shook my head, not wanting to decipher at the moment the one thing I could never really figure out. Me.

* * * *

I watched as Jessica and Michael talked to each other through the wall. They couldn't see each other, but they could hear each other's voices. They talked about the perfected and their immense importance and superiority. They talked about the flawed and their twisted minds. They talked about the humans and their diminished worth. They talked about Drew, the crazy girl who said she knew them.

I stayed in the shadows, certain they couldn't see me, and watched for any signs of the people they had previously been. Of course, I saw none.

Suddenly my mind wandered back to God. I looked at Jessica through the shadows, just staring. Was God going to bring her back? I didn't know. That realization hurt, but it was true. I knew why I had been feeling so empty, so lost, so alone. Jessica was my anchor to God.

And my anchor was gone.

Chapter Fourteen

I didn't know why I spent so much time downstairs watching Jessica and Michael. What did I expect? Nothing. Deep down, I knew they weren't coming back. At least not any time soon. I had noticed little differences in me. How I hadn't cried in over a week. That was a plus. For the first time, I hadn't cried about Michael when I was alone late at night in my tent. I hadn't cried about Jessica either. Or Yvonne. I was slowly morphing into a girl who no longer cared. Who no longer cared about what more could happen because everything I had loved was gone and nothing else mattered. At times when I felt discouraged, I reminded myself that this made me stronger, and I began to believe it. It was like being numb. At first you felt the cold, it stung, you cried, you tried to get rid of it, but eventually it took over, and there was nothing left to feel.

Michael was fiddling with something in the corner of his cell. The sound of scratching clawed at my ears as he scraped a rock against the stone floor. Over and over again. I couldn't tell what he was doing because I was too far away. He looked up, and we held each other's gaze for a moment before he turned and went back to scratching the floor.

He was used to me now. They both were. Jessica and Michael knew that I frequently spent my time watching them, and after a while, they stopped caring. I used to talk to them until I found out it was no good. I didn't know why I just sat here, staring at them. Maybe because every time I walked away, I kept forgetting what they were really like. Sitting here staring at them reminded me, every second, that Jessica and Michael were gone. I didn't like pretending or tricking myself. I was done with that.

"What are you doing?" I asked standing up, afraid that Michael might be creating some weapon or means of escape. He turned to look at me and held up the rock as if to show he had nothing. I stared at the floor, and all I saw were some scratch marks on the stone.

"Just finding a way to spend my time," he answered and then went back to what he had been doing. The rock was small and the scrapes were shallow so I thought nothing of it and went back to my chair near the doorway. Jessica was watching me with an expression very unlike the old Jessica. Her eyes followed me with a hungry stare that narrowed every time I glanced her way.

Suddenly Michael got up from his spot in the floor and walked to the front of his cell, his eyes wide. I frowned in confusion when I noticed Jessica was doing the same thing. Suddenly Michael started shaking the bars and pounding on the wall.

I stood up, alarmed. "What are you doing?" I asked, walking toward them. Jessica started yelling at me and kicking the door. "Stop," I ordered both of them. Michael was shaking his head, and Jessica was making frustrated noises when she couldn't penetrate the cell. The sound of clanking metal, pounding, and shrieking was starting to blur into an overwhelming noise. I reached out to grab the bars that Michael was pounding when my gaze was averted to his arm. He had been repeatedly pounding the wall with the same fist and the skin had been scraped away, leaving blood and metal exposed. "Stop!" I said again, looking at him. Michael didn't even look at me. It was as if he couldn't hear. I heard him mutter something, but it was more like a cry than any words I could understand. Their lack of attention was starting to scare me.

I hurried over to Jessica's cell and grabbed her arms through the bars. She struggled for a second and then went still, her eyes wide, although I wasn't sure why. "Why are you doing this?" I asked. She let out a small, strangled moan and started shaking her head. I let go of her arms, and she went back to hitting and shaking the door. I backed away from the cells and watched them. They hadn't even acknowledged me.

Suddenly, just as soon as it had started, they stopped kicking and yelling. Michael's shoulders relaxed and he calmly wiped his hand on his jeans, leaving a smear of blood. Jessica blinked a few times before returning to her sitting position on the ground.

I watched as Michael went back to scraping the floor with a stone as if nothing had happened. Why would they start yelling and trying to break free and then immediately go back to being calm? And at the exact same time? I frowned, watching them.

Just then an image flashed through my mind; a memory of Yvonne explaining the newer androids. Explaining about their minor programming. The realization dawned on me. Jessica and Michael had been programmed. The pieces swirled together in my mind, trying to fit together, to complete the puzzle.

The creators must have ordered them to escape, but they couldn't.

I hurriedly left the room, sprinted up the stairs and dashed outside toward Cassandra's tent. When I entered, I found her sitting at the table fiddling with some piece of electronic equipment I couldn't identify. Before Cassandra had even had time to say hello I had blurted out my new discovery. "They're programmed," I said.

Cassandra looked at me for a second, as if processing the information. "Programmed? Are you sure?" she asked.

I nodded. "I remember Yvonne telling me once about how the newer androids, only the new ones, have minor programming. Basically, they have a mind of their own, but the creators can override it any time they want." Cassandra frowned in concentration. "I forgot all about it until I saw Michael and Jessica just freak out. All of a sudden they were up and trying to get out. They weren't thinking," I explained.

Cassandra nodded. "I didn't know they were programmed," she said slowly. "None of us really were. So we just assumed the newer androids were like us."

"They must be controlled through the creators' computers," I went on, "since that's how things are originally programmed. So there must be a possibility of bringing them back to their personalities."

Cassandra looked thoughtful for a moment and then nodded. "It would make sense," she said. "We just have no idea how they're doing it or how to get to their computers and hack into them…" she trailed off. "We need an inside man."

An inside man. Where would we find an inside man? Everyone at the flawed camp was on the creators' list for extermination. I sighed.

"But don't give up," Cassandra said. "We can try to find a way."

Chapter Fifteen

I watched as the trees flew by the window and listened to the car's steady hum as we drove down the long dirt path. Beatrix was driving, trying to avoid potholes in the road, and causing us to jerk around in the car.

We had recently been the appointed team to go grocery shopping whenever supplies were needed, and I couldn't say I minded; any distraction from Michael and Jessica was a good thing.

"So I heard you and Cassandra have some other theory on how to bring the perfected back?" Beatrix asked me, turning slightly to look at me.

"I found out that the newer androids are programmed; well, I remembered, actually. Anyway, it won't work unless we have someone on the inside working with us," I told her sadly.

Beatrix shrugged. "I don't know, Cassandra's pretty computer savvy. I wouldn't underestimate her," she said with a smile.

I smiled back, but didn't fully believe her. Hope was one thing I was having a hard time keeping a hold of lately.

The car rolled along, and before I knew it, Beatrix was pulling into the grocery store parking lot. We hopped out of the car and made our way to the front doors. We had a habit of trying to look inconspicuous, so we kept our heads bent as we entered. We wandered around the store grabbing non-perishable items like canned goods and a few bags of chips. Overstocking was one thing the flawed were very into practicing. The fewer times anyone had to leave camp, the better.

Beatrix and I stood in the checkout line, waiting for our turn. I grabbed a magazine and started randomly flipping through pages. My eyes caught one of the headlines and I quickly turned back to the page.

"A New World", it read. "Good or Bad?" There was a photo beneath the headline of a particularly beautiful android woman. I knew this was going to have to be publicly addressed at some point, but everything was moving so fast. I skimmed over the article, finding that mass amounts of people were fleeing the country, but the article also assured everyone that being perfected was not a bad thing, and nothing bad would happen to you. Something I knew to be a lie. Something I knew to be written by one of the creators.

"Being perfected does not change you. It simply enhances your natural abilities."

My stomach was starting to churn. Lies. They were lying. Suddenly a new thought occurred to me. Were they really changing people's minds with articles like these? Were people actually willingly going to the creators and asking to be perfected? Asking to be turned into something they had no idea was far from what the creators told them it would be?

Beatrix leaned over to see what I was reading, and her brow furrowed. She glanced up, and our eyes met. We didn't need words to tell each other what we were thinking.

I put the magazine back, and we quickly checked out. Both of our hands were full as we left the store and started scanning the parking lot for where we had left our car. Beatrix spotted it, and we headed in that direction.

Suddenly I heard Beatrix scream my name, and I looked up just in time to see a large SUV slam into my side. I let out a shriek as I rolled up onto the windshield, the groceries spilling out of the bags and hitting the ground around the car. I felt the windshield crack beneath me, but I barely had time to register what had happened before the car swiftly backed up and I went rolling off and onto the hard, paved ground. A sharp pain raced through the side of my head, and I felt something warm and sticky trickling down my face. I looked in the direction the car had gone and stared in shock when I saw that it was racing my way again. I quickly rolled out of the way, the car barely scraping my side.

The SUV came to a halt, and two androids jumped out. I heard Beatrix shout as one of them pulled me roughly to my feet. I punched him as hard as I could in the face and took off running. I met up with Beatrix, and we ran about ten feet before the androids caught up. I felt one grab my arm and swing me around, and the other one grabbed me as well. I looked at them in surprise, noticing that they were only trying to get to me and they were willing to let Beatrix go. I only let myself have a second of confusion before looking for her.

She stood a few feet away, ready to attack the androids, but my voice stopped her. "No," I yelled, knowing that they probably had guns or other means of stopping her. "Go!"

She hesitated, giving me a puzzled look. "Go!" I screamed again as the female android turned to look at her. The other one shoved me to the ground.

Beatrix gave me one last look, a firm, determined glance, and ran off. I knew that look. She was going for help.

I turned and tried to kick the android that was holding me, but he held a firm grip on my arm and twisted it painfully upwards.

"You're that one android," the female said, looking at me. "The naughty one; the one that betrayed her father," she said with a smirk.

"Father...?" I started to say, but was cut off as the male android hit me across the face with something hard and metallic. I fell to the ground with a gasp of pain, feeling blood sliding over my eyelids. I blinked and wiped it away.

"You know you're on the list to be executed," the male android told me. "We'll get a nice reward for you."

I heard the click of the hammer of a pistol and, without looking up to see them, I wondered if they were going to kill me right here or if they were just going to use it to get me back to the Institution. I stared at my hands which were planted firmly on the ground, keeping me stable in my crouching position.

"Get up."

I felt the barrel being pressed firmly against the back of my neck. Stupid. You never get that close to the person you are threatening, especially if you don't really plan on shooting them. Even *I* knew that.

Before they could make a move, I had swirled around, grabbed the gun, yanked it from his hand, and pointed it at the man's face. He stared at me with alarm as I slowly got up from the ground, although a little unsteadily.

I stood a few feet away from them, the gun pointed at their eye level. I stood there for a moment, unsure of what to do. I started to back slowly away.

"They'll get you," the female said mockingly. "Running won't do any good."

I glared at her. *Shoot them,* something in my mind told me. My breath caught in my throat and I frowned, startled that I would think of something like that. I watched them for a moment, and the idea slowly started to get better and better. *They'll just follow me,* I told myself. How would I get away? *Shoot them.*

My hand was sweating, and I stared into their eyes, daring them to make a move.

Shoot them.

The girl watched me carefully while the other just stood there. He glared into my eyes as if daring me to pull the trigger. *Do it,* he seemed to say.

I was breathing hard, my heart was racing, my head was throbbing, I wanted out. I wanted to get away. *Shoot them!*

No. I pulled my finger away from the trigger. These were people. No matter how far their personalities were suppressed, they were still there. I couldn't kill people. I couldn't kill anyone. "I won't stoop to your level," I said under my breath, and I doubted they could hear me.

And then I turned and ran.

Chapter Sixteen

I knew they would follow me if they thought they could catch me, so I ran as fast as I could across the parking lot and down the street. I couldn't hear any signs of them coming after me, but pain throbbed through my head and there was a steady pounding in my ears, making it difficult to hear anything at all.

I raced across the pavement and into the trees where the dirt road led to the flawed camp. I stayed in the midst of the forest, while keeping the road in sight. I didn't want the androids to know exactly where I was. I didn't even know if they were following, but I couldn't take that chance.

I ran blindly through the woods. My head felt like it was going to explode, and the bleeding was getting worse. Blood was pouring down my face from where I had been hit across the forehead, and I had to wipe it away before it blinded my vision. I felt lightheaded, and I was starting to get nauseous. I stumbled to my knees and gasped in air, but only for a second before I forced myself up and started running again.

The sight of my bloodstained hands and shirt only made my stomach churn more. *How badly am I bleeding?* I wondered vaguely. Was I really hurt that badly? I had heard somewhere that head wounds tended to bleed a lot, but this seemed more than just a lot.

If I were a human, I would probably be dead, I thought. The thought made me sick to my stomach. Would they have killed me if I hadn't taken their gun?

The gun. Suddenly I remembered that I was holding it in my hand, and I squeezed it tighter.

But what would I do with a gun out here? What use would this be unless the androids had decided to follow me? *Did they follow me? Why didn't they kill me in the first place?* I started slowing down. I was tired. I wasn't thinking. I needed to get back to camp. *But camp is so far away...*

The trees were starting to look fuzzy and wiggly. I squinted and stared at them again. *Trees aren't supposed to do that,* I thought, but I didn't seem to care. Suddenly my knees gave out, and I fell to the ground. I let out a cry of frustration and gripped the ground beneath me. *Get up! Get up...*

My arms were tingling. Everything was spinning. *Trees don't spin,* I thought. I don't remember falling again, but suddenly the side of my face was pressed to the dirt beneath me. I stared into the spinning forest until the blood oozing from my forehead forced me to close my eyes.

The last thing I saw was red.

Chapter Seventeen

The first thing I was aware of was a pounding ache in my head. I heard a weird, garbled noise and suddenly realized that it had come from me. I moaned again and slowly opened my eyes. A bright, searing light shot pain through my skull, and I squeezed my eyes shut again.

"Drew?" a soft voice asked.

I moaned again.

"She's awake," I heard the voice say. I recognized it as Marian's.

I heard footsteps and sensed that more people had approached me. I heard Cameron's voice quietly telling me to try and open my eyes. I slowly opened them, squinting at the brightness. I looked up to see the faces of Marian, Cameron, and Beatrix standing over me. They looked blurry at first, but slowly focused to clarity.

"Can you see us okay?" Cameron asked.

I nodded stiffly. I tried to speak, but realized my throat was dry. I made a strange, raspy noise. Marian hurried to the sink in the corner and poured me a glass of water. I chugged it down, nearly choking on it as I felt the water soothingly slide down my throat.

I looked around. I was in the medical room back at the flawed camp. I breathed a sigh of relief.

"I'm so glad you're okay," Beatrix said quietly. "What happened?"

"They hit me," I replied, although my voice still sounded odd.

"With something hard, by the looks of you," Cameron added.

I nodded. "A gun."

Marian's jaw dropped. "A gun?" She gave me a quizzical look. "Why would they *hit* you with it?"

"I don't think they intended on actually killing me."

"We found you a ways from the road," Beatrix said. "We've been searching all night."

Just then I noticed how tired and stressed they all looked, and I felt a rush of gratitude. "Thank you," I managed to say.

"The gun you had in your hand," Cameron started to say. "Is that the gun they hit you with?"

I nodded. "I took it from them and ran." I pressed my hand to my forehead, hoping to lessen the pain.

"Don't touch it," Cameron said quickly, pulling my hand away. "You'll make it worse."

I sighed. "So when can I leave?"

Cameron gave me an amused look and shook his head. "Not for a day or two." I opened my mouth to protest, but he beat me to it. "At least overnight," he added.

I closed my mouth. My head did hurt a lot. Maybe it *would* be best if I stayed here for awhile.

"You'll be fine as long as you just take it easy for a few days," Cameron told me. "I gotta go tell some people you're okay," he added and left the room.

"Cassandra's been going nuts all morning," Beatrix told me. "We were the ones who found you."

I was silent.

Beatrix shifted uncomfortably. "When we saw you from a distance with the gun in your hand and blood all over the place," she paused, a grim expression on her face. "We thought—we thought you were dead."

I thought back on how I had collapsed in the forest. I probably had looked dead. I didn't know how much blood I had lost, but if there was enough to be blinding my vision every few seconds there must have been quite a lot.

Just then Cassandra came bursting into the room. "Drew!" she cried, running to the bed and flinging her arms around me.

I laughed in spite of the pain and hugged her back.

"I'm so glad you're okay!" Cassandra exclaimed.

"I'm fine," I assured her.

"What happened?" she asked in concern. She leaned back to a

standing position.

"Androids came in a car," I told her.

"She got hit with it too," Beatrix added.

Cassandra's expression turned to horrified shock. "Did they shoot you?" she asked quickly.

I shook my head. "They just hit me with the barrel," I pointed to my forehead.

Cassandra's eyes widened. "Geez, Drew," she said with a smile. "You're indestructible."

I half-smiled back. "Made that way."

Chapter Eighteen

I stared down at the blue blanket that lay over my legs. It was a sky blue; almost the color of my eyes. I had specifically asked them to bring me the blanket I had been using in my tent instead of the white ones they had originally given me. I didn't like white anymore. It reminded too much of the Institution. The blue made me feel like a real person; like someone who had a favorite color.

I heard the door open and looked up to see Marian enter the room. "How are you feeling today?" she asked me.

"Better." My head hurt much less than it had the day before, and I was beginning to think clearer as well.

"That's good," she said with a smile, sitting down in the chair beside my bed.

"Still a little stiff," I admitted.

"You'll feel better soon," she assured me.

I nodded. "There was something weird about when they attacked me though," I told her slowly.

Marian raised her eyebrows in expectation.

"They didn't try to get Beatrix," I told Marian. "They were trying primarily to just get me." I watched Marian, trying to read her expression.

Her brows furrowed. "They only tried to get you?"

I nodded. "At least that's how it seemed…"

"Beatrix wouldn't be in line with them." Marian said. It wasn't a defensive statement, just a fact. We both knew Beatrix wasn't the kind to betray us for the creators. She was too involved with our cause;

something you couldn't fake easily.

"I know," I told her. "I didn't think that because I knew she wouldn't ever do anything like that."

Marian nodded slowly. "The creators must want you for some reason. They must want you more than the others."

I was silent; thinking. "But why am I so special?" I asked no one in particular. "What sets me apart from all the other flawed?" Why didn't they just shoot me?

Marian was staring at me with a thoughtful expression, as if she didn't know what to make of me. "Maybe it has something to do with you not remembering anything before you were perfected?"

I shrugged. "You think those two things could be connected?"

"Well those are two things that set you apart from the other flawed," she said. "I'm just thinking out loud."

We sat there for a moment in silence; each lost in our own thoughts. "I wish they would just … just…" I clenched my fists at my sides, trying to find the right words.

Marian just nodded. "I know," she said quietly.

"I'm so sick of them doing this to us!" I said forcefully. Marian was quiet. "They've ruined our lives. I hate them for what they've done to everyone." My voice was rising.

"Drew," Marian said, but I ignored her.

"They've taken *everything* from me!" I cried, pushing back the tears that were threatening to spill out of my eyes. "I have nothing left!" My fists were clenched, and I was shaking with anger.

"Drew," Marian said again, and I looked over to meet her gaze. Her sympathy was gone but there was still a kind look in her eyes. "I know you've been through a lot," she said quietly. "But we're all going through hard times. We've all lost people."

There was a moment of silence. I just watched her.

"You have not lost everything," she said firmly. "God would not let you lose everything. He wouldn't give you more than you could handle."

I shook my head, not wanting to hear this. "But He did!" I cried. "Why did He let Jessica and Michael *die?*" I was shouting although my anger wasn't intended to be directed at Marian; she was just in the way.

"Drew they're not—"

"They're just as good as dead!" I nearly screamed at her. "They're not coming back."

Marian stood up. "Drew, you are *alive,*" she nearly spat. "You should be dead, but you aren't. God wants you alive because you're meant to do something, and you need to see that."

I was shaking my head. "I don't want any part in it," I replied, staring down at my hands.

Marian frowned at me. "I know you don't want to hear this, but you have to," she said sadly. "You need to stop feeling sorry for yourself. That's not going to help you. You need to deal with what you have and be thankful for what you've got, not what you've lost."

There was a tense pause.

"I know it's hard," she said, "and after you've lost everything else, like you said, how can you purposefully lose sight of the one thing that could comfort you?" she asked me. Her voice wasn't accusatory, it was just sad.

I was frowning at my hands.

She shook her head. "We all need something to lean on, Drew," she said and then she left.

Chapter Nineteen

I thought about God. I hadn't thought about God in a long time. I had purposefully trained my mind to block Him out. I was angry. Angry at everything. I wasn't sure what I was doing. I wasn't forming thoughts in my head, trying to find reasons for what had happened to me or wondering why God would let it happen; I was just thinking.

Does God care about me? I let myself wonder. I didn't answer the question. I just let it hang there until it slowly faded away.

It was a few days after my fight with Marian, and we hadn't spoken since. Mostly, because I had been avoiding her. What could I say? We couldn't ignore the conversation we'd had. It wouldn't just disappear.

I left my tent and wandered off toward the building where Jessica and Michael were being kept. I trudged down the stairs and saw both of their heads turn in my direction to stare at me as I walked in. I sat down on the last step and propped my elbows up on my knees, leaning into my hands.

I watched them. They stared suspiciously at me for a moment before looking away. Michael was scraping the ground in the corner as he did every day, and I was starting to wonder if he was slowly going insane. I couldn't blame him. Cells were terrible. I knew. Jessica spent most of her time just sitting there, staring up at the window in the hallway. From her viewpoint, I knew she couldn't see much; just sky and anything that happened to be passing by from a great height, like birds or bugs. But it was better than staring at the wall.

* * * *

I sat alone in the large game room, my glance skittering along the spines of books that lined the bookshelves. I was sitting in one of the cushioned chairs placed there for reading. My legs were curled under me as I studied the titles. I looked out the window across the room and saw a leaf falling from one of the trees outside. It twirled slowly and gracefully until it vanished beneath the windowsill.

I turned my attention back to the books. I grabbed one and started randomly skimming through it. I barely stopped to read a few words before I would turn the page again. I didn't take the book for something to read, but for something to keep my restless hands busy. I was flipping through the pages so quickly now that I barely had time to read even one word. They flashed through my mind and then were gone, replaced by the new one. Sincerely. Glanced. Where. Betrayed. He. Gone. Why. Love.

I slammed the book shut. I quickly placed it back on the shelf and left the room. I was breathing heavily, and I wasn't even sure why. Thoughts of Michael flashed through my mind, and I squeezed my eyes shut, willing them to go away. Yvonne had also taken a habit of haunting my dreams and mind as well.

I shoved the door open, feeling the cold sting of the autumn breeze against my skin, blowing a strand of hair in my face. I reached up to brush it out of the way.

The flawed camp was surrounded by trees in every direction, and I ran blindly into the midst of them. I didn't know where I was going; all I knew was I that I wanted to get away from here. If only for a minute, I just wanted to get away.

I ran faster, jumping over debris or shrubbery in my way, pushing branches back as I ran through. My breath was coming out in uneven gasps, but I ran faster. I knew the forest was deathly silent, but it seemed to be alive and thundering as I bolted by. All I was aware of was the incessant pounding of my footsteps on the forest floor, my loud, labored breathing, and the beating of my heart.

I ran faster. I knew no human could run this fast, but I knew the newer androids could run faster. I ordered my legs to speed up, all the sounds suddenly humming into a wildly quick and frenzied scream. *You will not beat me,* I thought. *I can be better.* I thought of Michael. Of his laughing eyes and his beautiful smile, replaced by the android he had become. I thought of the other androids; the new ones. The ones with no heart, no emotions, no nothing. *Not Michael,* I thought.

I ran faster.

Not fair.

My lungs hurt. My feet hurt. My heart was beating so fast I thought it might break.

Not Jessica.

I thought of her deep brown eyes, intelligent, caring.

Not Yvonne.

A memory flashed through my mind. Yvonne and I as kids. Her eyes sparkling as we laughed.

I ran faster.

You're perfect Drew. Perfect, Glen's voice rang in my mind. *Perfect.*

"No!" I screamed, coming to a halt. The momentum sent me stumbling to the ground. Everything was quiet, and my heavy breathing seemed too loud. The silence was serene, and I felt like an intruder for breaking it because my heart was racing, pounding against my chest, yearning to break free. My breathing came out in gasps and I clenched leaves together in my fists. A sound escaped my throat; not a word, just a scream.

"I will not be what you made me to be!" I screamed. "I will not be perfect!" I was sobbing now, although I wasn't even sure why. Tears were streaming down my face and everything hurt. Not just my head. Not just the places where the car had hit. But everything; everything inside of me; my heart, my soul, my mind. They throbbed and stung, screaming for the one thing I had pushed away.

"Help me," I said; quieter this time, although it came out in a forceful sob. "God, help me." I heard sobs and gasps for air that I couldn't believe were coming out of my own mouth. "I can't do it anymore." I was shaking my head. "I can't do this alone!"

I sat there, on my hands and knees as my crying slowly diminished and a sudden calm enveloped me. "I'm sorry," I whispered.

I closed my eyes and tried to steady my breathing. "Help me," I said again.

And this time, beyond a shadow of a doubt, I knew that He heard me.

Chapter Twenty

I slowly walked back to camp. It took me longer since I had basically sprinted the whole way through, but it was better to walk; I had time to think.

Suddenly I heard noises and I knew I was close to camp. I started to pick up the pace when I heard angry and anxious voices. I darted through the trees and into the dirt driveway.

In the center of the clearing stood a large group of people huddled around something I couldn't see. I quickly made my way toward them. One of the flawed turned around to see who was coming and her expression morphed into shock. I frowned in confusion. Was there a problem? A few people shifted out of the way and what I saw made me stop dead in my tracks.

I froze. Yvonne looked up and our eyes met. I stared at her, and she just stared back. *She's supposed to be dead,* my mind kept telling me. I shook my head. But she wasn't. A small smile slowly crept across my face. I didn't know why I was smiling. All I could think about was the fact that Yvonne was alive. I didn't even know if that was a good or a bad thing, but I knew that I had never wanted her dead.

I walked toward her, wiping the smile off my face in case Yvonne mistook it for some other meaning. "Yvonne," I said.

"Drew," she said, amusement dancing in her eyes. She acted as if she had the upper hand. Yvonne was good at her mind games. She always had been.

I turned toward the person who was holding her, a question in my expression.

"We found her close to the camp," he explained. "We thought she was a spy sent from the Institution."

I nodded in understanding. I turned back to Yvonne. "I thought the creators were going to kill you," I said. I hadn't meant for the words to sound so harsh, but killing in any sentence sounded harsh, and I needed to ask the question.

Yvonne looked away, and I was surprised. Yvonne was never the first to lose eye contact. Had the creators really broken Yvonne? Fearless Yvonne?

She shrugged. "Yeah." She forced an indifferent tone.

There was a pause, and I realized I had never seen Yvonne this vulnerable. She was like a child. A child who had been crushed. "I'm sorry," I said quietly. Because I knew what it was like to be crushed.

"I don't need your sympathy," she replied. It wasn't a harsh answer, just a tired statement. "You need it more than I do," she whispered. My mouth partially opened in shock. Was that regret I saw in her eyes? But then she looked away.

"We're going to take her to answer some questions and then lock her up with the others," one of the flawed said.

"Okay," I managed to utter. I watched as Yvonne was led away. She was almost like a different person; a little less cocky and a little more humble. But maybe that was just because she had been captured. I frowned in thought. Yvonne was too smart to let herself be caught that easily. If she had really been sent here by the creators she wouldn't have been so tacky. There had to be some other reason she was here.

But what?

I watched until they all disappeared inside the building, and I walked away. I headed toward the other house where Michael and Jessica were kept. If only I could talk to them; the only other people who knew what Yvonne was like as well as I did. If only they were still there to talk to.

I entered the room and walked to my seat across from the cells. Jessica was standing, a sight that caught my attention since she was normally sitting in the corner and rarely did she ever get up. At first I thought that she might be going off on one of those crazy programming fits but then my gaze met hers. There was something in her eyes;

recognition? My heart filled with hope and I stood, frozen to the spot, hoping, praying that my suspicion was right, but not daring to move in case I might break the spell. Jessica's expression slowly faded into a smile.

"Drew."

Chapter Twenty-one

I stood there for a moment, shocked. Had Jessica really just said my name? We stared at each other for a moment and a smile slowly spread across her face. A real smile. Jessica's real smile. I ran to the cell, unlocking it as fast as I could, and collided into Jessica's arms. She was taller than the last time I had hugged her, and more firmly built. But she was still Jessica. I felt tears prickling the corners of my eyes, and I had the suspicion that Jessica was fighting back tears as well. I started laughing so I wouldn't cry and so did Jessica.

"You remember," I barely managed to say. We pulled apart and left the cell. Jessica nodded and smiled. "I don't know why. I just—all of a sudden ... it was *you*." She shrugged again and laughed. "I can't believe I didn't remember earlier..." she trailed off, but the smile still remained on her face. We stood there for a moment, just looking at each other; smiling and sometimes laughing. Suddenly she looked up and an urgent and excited expression on her face. "Kyle," she said quietly.

I smiled. Suddenly Jessica was running, and I was running after her. I heard shouts from across the clearing once we had reached outside, but I quickly waved them away with an explanation of, "She's back!"

I saw Kyle emerging from one of the tents, and at the sight of Jessica he stopped, his eyes widening. He looked to me for confirmation, and I nodded. He didn't need to wait for anything more. Kyle sprinted across the clearing and so did Jessica. They collided into a hug. Kyle lifted Jessica partially off the ground as he swung her in a circle then put her back down. Somewhere in the mess of hugging and laughing, their lips met, and I watched them kissing each other as if they were never going to stop. After a moment of watching them, I began to think that that was their intention. I tried to suppress a laugh, and finally, they pulled away from each other. Jessica was beaming and both of them were laughing.

I walked over to them. Jessica was holding firmly onto Kyle's hand, and they looked like they might never let go. I smiled at them, feeling something in my heart start to fill up; a place that had been empty for too long.

"So what's new?" Jessica laughed. Her eyes sparkled, a genuine smile on her face. I hadn't even realized how much I had missed her; how much of an influence she was on my life. I didn't want to cry, so I laughed instead. Jessica was back.

"We have a lot to catch up on," I replied.

* * * *

"She must know how to fix the perfected," Cassandra insisted. "She was a co-leader of the Institution." Her eyes bore urgently into mine. We were sitting in her tent, her various tools lay strewn across the floor, and a lamp hung precariously from the ceiling, sending an eerie glow throughout the room.

I held out my hands helplessly. "I don't know," I admitted. "She looks like she's gone through a lot, and I don't even know if she knows."

"Drew!" Cassandra exclaimed exasperatedly.

"You don't know Yvonne," I shot back. "Just subtle movements that she did today—she would never have dreamed of doing things like that. Something happened to her. I'm not saying I won't ask, I'm just saying it might be best to wait."

Cassandra heaved a sigh of frustration.

"If Yvonne is upset, she's not going to spill anything," I added.

Cassandra drummed her fingers on the table. I sighed as well. I was tired. We had ended up putting Yvonne in the cell next to Michael's, much to her alarm. I had tried talking to her only a few times; not about anything in particular, just talk, but she hadn't even said a word. For some reason, I knew talking to her was urgent. I didn't know why. But something was coming.

"I don't think we have time to waste, Drew," Cassandra said tiredly.

"Everything is moving so fast, we need information and we need it as soon as possible." She looked at me, her piercing blue eyes searching mine for a sign of agreement. "Just try."

I bit my lip. *Just try.* Those words were easier said than done. But I knew Cassandra was right. There really was no time to waste. I ran my fingers through my hair, a movement I had begun to associate with stress. This small movement made me think of Michael and the way he had always used to do the same thing.

I stood up. "I'll try," I told her wearily.

* * * *

Yvonne sat at the front of her cell, staring ahead at the wall across the hallway. Her hair was beginning to grow out, I noticed. It almost reached her shoulders. Her eyes seemed less expressive, less bright, and less alive.

"Yvonne?" I said quietly. She didn't look up. I slid the chair across the floor so that it was in front of Yvonne's cell. I sat down. "I don't know why you won't talk to me," I told her. "I'm not..." I threw my hands into the air helplessly, "trying to hurt you or get you hurt." There was a long silence. Yvonne still didn't even look at me. I leaned forward so that my face was inches from the bars. "Please," I said, "the creators tried to kill you; you have no ties to them anymore. Help us."

Yvonne glanced up, her eyes dark and angry. "I don't think I can do that, Drew." Her voice sounded strained and hesitant, but her eyes were steady and calm.

"Why?" I pressed. "Why do you feel like you owe them?" Yvonne looked away. "We're not your enemy anymore!" I went on. "They are."

Suddenly Yvonne looked up. Her eyes had lost their anger and in them was just curiosity. "I will not tell you," she said firmly. I frowned. Her expression didn't match the tone of her voice.

I stood up. "Fine," I said quietly. I turned to walk away but took one look back. Yvonne was staring at me. Her lips were pursed together, and her eyes pinned me to the spot. I stared back. Her eyes were speaking to me; telling me the things that her mouth couldn't.

But what were they saying?

Chapter Twenty-two

I was back with Yvonne the next day. Part of me wanted to go back, but part of me didn't. Not after what she had said. The tone of her voice had told me that Yvonne wanted nothing to do with me or any of the flawed. Her words had hurt, but something had kept nagging at me to return. It was her eyes. Her eyes had pulled me back. They had been filled with something I had never seen in her before.

What had they been saying?

I walked into the room, and Yvonne looked up when I came in; her face was expressionless. I sat down in the chair next to her cell, and we just sat there for a moment, watching each other. I took in a deep breath. "Why won't you help us?" I had the urge to ask. I asked it quietly, conscious of Michael in the other cell.

"I will not betray my creators." She said the words like she had rehearsed them a thousand times, but deep down she didn't really mean it. I frowned because, like yesterday, what her mouth was saying and what her eyes were saying were not the same. Her words had been stiff, and her eyes stared me down hungrily.

"Yvonne?" I asked warily, unsure of what to do.

Her eyes widened, and she ever so slightly shook her head. I gave her a questioning look. She pointed to her neck. I looked but saw nothing. I frowned in confusion.

"I don't—"

Yvonne started shaking her head so violently that I stopped abruptly. She looked around the room, almost frantic, and finally spotted a small rock. I backed away, unsure of what she was going to do with it. To my surprise, she started scratching on the wall. Letters began to form.

Injection, she wrote. *Hearing you.* She turned to look at me, her eyes staring at me more intensely than ever. And suddenly, what they said made sense.

I stood up so quickly the chair almost toppled over, and I held in a gasp of alarm.

The creators could hear us. Instead of killing Yvonne, they had sent her as a spy, equipped with recording software and most likely a tracking device. I was frozen. What could I do? Yvonne was already here; the creators had to know where we were by now. And what had her recording device picked up?

Yvonne made a writing motion with her hands and then gave me a pointed look. I nodded and mouthed the words, *Be right back.*

I quietly left the room and then raced across the clearing. In my tent were pencils and paper, and I quickly grabbed them before returning to Yvonne's cell.

I hurried down the hallway. I briefly glanced at Michael, seeing him scratching away in the corner again, and I shook my head, dismissing his odd behavior as pure boredom or something like that.

I reached through the bars of Yvonne's cell, handing her the paper and pencil. She immediately started writing. I stood there for a moment while Yvonne quickly scribbled words onto the faded notebook paper. After a minute she looked up and handed it back.

They can hear everything, but they can't see. They sent me here to get information. They know where you are, but they're waiting to see what you'll do.

I read the note quickly and then scribbled something back. *Are they coming?* My heart was racing, my head was pounding; I wanted to ask all these questions so quickly. Writing them out seemed to take forever, and I wasn't patient enough to wait the extra seconds that ticked by while we wrote our replies.

Yvonne shook her head. She tapped her finger on a word that she had already written; *waiting.*

Waiting. But for what? I started writing again.

Can you tell me about how to fix the perfected? I handed her the note. Once she saw it her expression melted into a slight frown. She looked up at me and shrugged; not the tantalizing, indifferent shrug I had seen her use many times before, but this one was truly from uncertainty. She took the pencil and started writing back.

Through the computers, she wrote. I nodded, trying to tell her that I already knew.

But can you tell us how to fix them? I pressed.

She shook her head, and I felt my heart sink. I wanted to scream at her; to ask her why, to make her explain, to ask her if she knew of *any* way, but I was forced to silence; the creators, once again, were monitoring my every word.

Yvonne grabbed the paper and pencil back. *I can't explain how. Not enough paper.*

I stared quizzically at the note and gave her an incredulous look. I made a confused gesture with my hands. Yvonne only stared at me with an amused smirk on her face. I rolled my eyes. She started writing.

But if you take me there, I can fix them for you.

Chapter Twenty-three

I burst into Cassandra's tent, causing her to jerk up from what she had been doing. "Drew!" she exclaimed, startled.

I didn't wait for anything else; I didn't even care how loudly I said it, how upsetting the other news was, or anything else for that matter. I didn't care. "She can fix the perfected," I panted. "She can fix them," I cried again.

Cassandra's face spread into a pleased but curious grin. "How?" she asked. "Were we right?" She stood up from her seat, putting down her tools on the table.

I nodded. "Programming. She says if we take her there, she can do it." Cassandra's eyebrows furrowed ever so slightly. My smile faded a little. "What?" I asked.

"Drew, she could be lying," she suggested.

I immediately shook my head, but then was surprised to realize I hadn't even thought of that possibility. After all Yvonne had done to me, I hadn't thought about the possibility of her tricking me once again. I closed my mouth, which I had opened originally to protest.

"I'm not saying this is true, but I don't know her and if she's what you and some others have described her to be, I wouldn't be too quick to believe her," she added.

I looked away, wondering if Yvonne would lie to me. I shook my head; silly question. *Would* she lie? Yes. *Did* she lie? Unknown. I looked up to meet Cassandra's eyes, thinking.

"Let's go talk to her," Cassandra said and started to head out of the tent.

I quickly reached out to grab her arm. "No," I said. She stopped and gave me a quizzical look. "There's more that I need to tell you," I admitted.

Cassandra's eyebrows knit together in concern. "Something bad?" she guessed.

"Yeah," I replied slowly. Cassandra shifted her feet and cocked her head, waiting for my response. "The creators know where we are," I said quickly, watching as Cassandra's expression changed from mildly curious to horrified shock.

"They know," she uttered, her mouth open and her blue eyes wide.

I started shaking my head and held my hands up. "But they aren't coming. At least not right now. That's what Yvonne said," I told her.

"How? Why?" Cassandra put her hand over her mouth, then took it off, sat down then stood up again. "Explain," she eventually said.

I took a deep breath and told her the whole conversation I'd had with Yvonne. I explained to her about her recording software and tracking device and how we had to be careful of what we said around her. The whole time, Cassandra's expression seemed to get more and more scared.

"The tracking device," she said after a pause. "We need to disable it."

I shook my head vehemently. "No. The creators already know where we are. If we disable the tracking device, they'll know we've found them out."

Cassandra nodded and put her head in her hands. "Yeah," she admitted.

I started pacing back and forth in the tent.

Cassandra looked up. "Yvonne said they were waiting," she said. "Waiting for what?" Her eyes were filled with anxiety; an expression that seemed foreign to her face.

I shook my head. "I don't know. To see what we'll do, I guess."

Cassandra sighed. "We need to tell the others." I nodded. "We need to make a plan." She went on. "We don't have a lot of time if what Yvonne's been saying is true."

"I believe it's true," I told her. "I've never seen her act that way. She wasn't lying."

Cassandra let out a sigh of frustration. "How much time do we have?" she asked wearily.

I shook my head. "I don't know, not much."

* * * *

Half an hour later, we were searching out Beatrix and the others, in an attempt to alert them to what we'd learned. We found them in the medical tent, going over inventory.

Beatrix's face went white when she learned the news, and Cameron pursed his lips together in concern. "Are you sure?" Beatrix asked me.

"That's what Yvonne told me," I replied.

"And we don't want to take any chances," Cassandra added. "I say we believe her for the time being and figure out some way to deal with this."

Beatrix sat down on the bed and bit her lip in thought. There was a long silence where all we did was stand there and think. I could feel the fear in the air around us, and I closed my eyes, hoping, praying, for an answer.

Beatrix's eyes shot up to look at us, the piercing green of her irises freezing us to the spot in that alarming effect she could have on people. "We need to leave." She said quietly. "As soon as possible. The only way we're going to survive is if we leave *now*." Her eyes were sad, as if she would rather do anything else, but knew this was the only way.

Cameron slowly nodded his head, and although Cassandra said nothing, I knew she agreed as well. I looked at the floor, studying the wood flooring they had worked so hard to create. Cassandra kicked a table leg in frustration. "We worked so hard..." Her teeth were clenched, and her hands were balled into fists. "We started from *nothing* out here." She heaved a sigh and looked away.

"We'll just have to find another place," Beatrix said sadly. The room was in a tense silence, every one of us fighting our own battles against the creators and the burning hatred that was tearing us apart.

I looked around the room at each of them and the struggle that was seen clearly on each of their faces. I clenched my fists at my side, suddenly feeling strong. I would not let the creators beat me. Not again. "No," I said. They all looked up at me, their eyes searching mine questioningly. "I'm tired of running," I said evenly. "I'm tired of being afraid." I said the words quietly but forcefully, and somehow I knew they all had understood. They all knew what it was like to run and hide, to be fearful, and to be feared.

"I'm done with the creators," I said slowly. I looked up to meet their eyes, pleading for them to agree. "Aren't you?"

Chapter Twenty-four

I will not run anymore. I will not hide anymore. Those words swirled through my head with a mixture of fear and power. I knew those thoughts were dangerous. I knew the safe way out would be to run as Beatrix had suggested. But I felt like that was the coward's way of solving this problem. Running wouldn't fix anything; it would still be there when we returned. I held frantically onto the strength I had had when I had first said those words; the strength that I knew I couldn't go on without.

"We're going to fix them," I had heard myself saying. "The creators are done." I hadn't expected the reactions they had given me. I had expected hesitance and fear, but instead I was met with victorious smiles and ideas. Everyone else was done, too. The creators had taken too much.

* * * *

I was sitting in the game room, along with at least a dozen other androids, around the long table where I had surprisingly found myself at the head. Frightened and worrisome talk went around like a swarm of bees buzzing in everyone's ears. The creators were coming. And everyone knew it.

I looked around at the faces of the people I had been friends with over the past few months. Although I had always seen the sorrow hidden beneath their smiling faces, I had never seen it as apparent as now.

"So we're going to fix the perfected," Marian said. It wasn't a question, just a statement thrown out there for feedback. Murmurs filled the room, but reluctant or excited, I couldn't tell.

I nodded. "We need to," I said firmly. "We're the only ones who can."

"Drew's right," Beatrix's voice chimed in. "Think about it. There are the creators and their androids, the humans, and then us. Three different groups of people. The humans have no idea what's going on or how to stop it, so that leaves us."

There was a tense silence while everyone seemed to digest the idea. "And how are we going to stop them?" a voice called. I recognized the girl to be Tina, an android who helped Cameron out in the medical department a lot.

"We have Yvonne, and she knows how to fix the perfected," I explained. "She can hack into their computer system and dismantle their programming." I watched as the expressions around me turned to suspicion at the mention of Yvonne's name. Mumbles ran through the group and people started shaking their heads.

"Hey," Cassandra called above the noise; her voice loud and demanding. "What other choice do we have?" She fixed everyone with a steely stare. "We're running out of options. Either we let the creators come get us, we run away like cowards, or we use tools that we have to make this right." Her outburst was met with silence. People were staring at their hands or at each other, trying to decide. Jessica looked over from beside me and smiled; her soft brown eyes slightly enhanced but still the same Jessica's.

"I say we go with Drew's plan," she stated, still smiling. "What've we got to lose?" Her tone was cheerful but still seemed to convey the message of how desperate we really were.

"Vote," Cassandra commanded, her piercing blue eyes seeming to sear through everyone in the room. "Drew's plan?" She raised her arm and Jessica, Beatrix, Marian, and Cameron's quickly followed. Slowly I watched as arm after arm was raised and suddenly the tension was gone, replaced by a humble acceptance of duty. Faces watched mine, a slight smile dancing in their features.

"Drew's plan it is then," Cassandra said with a nod. She turned to look at me, her eyebrows raised in expectance. "So what's the first step to creating this wondrous idea?" she asked with a laughing smile.

I shrugged, suddenly aware that every eye in the room was on me. I felt my face growing red from the attention and stares. "Well, we'll need to make out details of what exactly we'll be doing, and we'll need a leader," I added. Cassandra immediately came to my mind, with her strong voice and demanding presence, and I looked over at her. "Who should it be?" I asked, giving her a meaningful look.

Cassandra's eyes widened, and her eyebrows rose in shock, but then her expression softened into an amused grin. I saw Beatrix and some of the other androids exchange looks, and I watched them, puzzled. Cassandra laughed softly, as if finding me funny in some way. "You, Drew," she said quietly. Her light blue eyes smiled into mine. "It's always been you."

Chapter Twenty-five

I was sitting with Yvonne in her cell, watching her dark eyes closely; watching as they stared back at me evenly. Yvonne never lost. Could I trust her? After all the times she'd betrayed me, time after time after time … could I trust her again? Could I really put everyone's lives in her hands and pray that Yvonne had changed? That Yvonne wasn't that backstabbing android anymore, but the little girl I had grown up with?

Can I trust you? I mouthed, staring at her.

She grinned and shrugged, her eyes glinting. I held in an exasperated sigh and rolled my eyes. I glared at her. She held out her hands in a 'what?' gesture and mouthed back, *Can you?* In her eyes danced a smile; a playful one, full of fun and adventure. Yvonne was just playing with me. She always had been.

I closed my eyes, prayed for the strength not to strangle Yvonne right on the spot, and reached into my pocket to pull out three pieces of notebook paper. Yvonne watched them hungrily as I handed her the explanation of our plan. Not the whole plan, but the start.

Her eyes devoured every word, skimming the paper so fast I was surprised she had actually had time to read everything. When she was done, she looked up with a smile on her face. I pointed to the place where her part was explained and gave her a questioning glance. *Can you do it?* my eyes asked.

She nodded.

I stood up and unlocked the door, motioning for her to follow. Her eyebrows rose in question as she followed me out. I handed her another piece of paper, explaining how I had gotten her a room inside one of the buildings since she was now a critical piece in our plan. Yvonne smiled contently as she read.

We walked up the stairs and headed down the hallway at the top. I opened a small room that was originally meant as a closet but was the best we could scrounge up. Yvonne disapprovingly surveyed the small room that could barely hold the bed and chair we had managed to squeeze in, but she eventually shrugged and situated herself on the cushions.

I grabbed a pen from my pocket and scribbled something onto a scrap of notebook paper. *I'll be back later to discuss details of the plan. Just sit tight.*

I pulled out a pair of keys and smiled apologetically at Yvonne. I hated to do this to her. At least this room had a bed and a tiny window; much better than the cell she had recently been in.

Yvonne gave me a look as if saying *do you really think that'll keep me in here?* She was eyeing the keys reproachfully.

I sighed. *They don't trust you,* I mouthed. *Yet.* Yvonne only frowned. *Better than the cell,* I scribbled onto the paper. *Took a lot of arguing to get this room.*

And with that, I left, locking the door behind me. I closed my eyes, praying Yvonne wouldn't leave. I *had* done a lot of arguing to get her that room. I didn't want my ally in our plan to be stuck in a cell downstairs. It just didn't seem right. But the only reason they had agreed to let me move her to a room was because they underestimated her. A locked door wouldn't stop Yvonne. Even a doubly lined locked door, like the one in her room.

I sighed. If she had wanted to leave, she would've by now. That's why I trusted her. You couldn't *make* her do anything. You couldn't control Yvonne.

Chapter Twenty-six

Sun shone through the tent, forcing my eyes open. I sat up and looked at my light-dappled sleeping bag. I rubbed my eyes and let out a slow sigh. I had been rushing nonstop the past few days, writing and rewriting plans, and had taken hardly any time at all to just relax. Last night I had reluctantly gone to sleep after much pressing from Cassandra and Jessica, telling me that I needed rest.

I let my legs fall over the side of my bed, glad they had talked me into sleeping, because I felt much more energized than I had in awhile. I stood up, running my fingers through my hair and quickly getting dressed into jeans and a T-shirt.

I walked out of the tent and looked around in surprise to see that, during the night, an inch of snow had blanketed the frozen ground, covering its ugliness until spring. I looked around at the white mantled trees and tents and headed toward the building where Yvonne was staying. I knocked on her door, and Yvonne's bored voice answered. I walked in to see her lying on the bed reading a magazine. She looked up and halfheartedly smiled when I came in.

I sat down in the chair and held out a box of chocolates I had brought with me from my tent. "You want some?" I asked her, shaking the box.

Yvonne frowned at me, her nose wrinkling. "I don't eat, Drew," she said snottily. "Never have. You know that." She went back to studying her magazine.

I wrinkled my nose at her and shrugged, popping a chocolate in my mouth. We sat there for a moment in silence while I chewed my candy.

"Well, I just wanted to say good morning," I told her, beginning to stand up.

"Yeah, whatever," Yvonne replied, pointing to her neck, reminding me once again that every word I said was being heard by the creators.

I gave her a knowing look and left the room. I stood out in the hallway for a moment, staring at the door I had just locked. I still had some doubt about Yvonne nagging me in the back of my mind. I frowned and tried to push it away; I had no time to wonder about her, I had no time to do anything. I just had to trust her. There was no alternative.

I started heading down the hallway and found myself going down the stairs that led to the cells where Michael was still being kept. I suddenly realized I hadn't seen Michael in quite awhile. I had been so preoccupied, I had stopped visiting him as frequently as I used to.

It was absolutely silent as I walked down the stairs; the only noise was the clicking of my shoes against the floor. I walked into the hallway and automatically headed for my chair across the cells, but something made me stop.

My heart began to race, my breathing stopped, my hands clenched at my sides. I forced myself to look again at what I had just barely glanced upon. Seeing it again only made my heart race faster.

The cell in which Michael had spent so much time was empty, the door hanging slightly ajar. I wanted to run. To run anywhere. To the cell, to the others, to the forest. But my legs were frozen; the blood in my veins had turned cold.

Michael gone? Again? My mind thought numbly. For some reason I couldn't comprehend this, but at the same time I wasn't really surprised.

I turned and ran from the room. I didn't know who I wanted to talk to. I didn't know which person I should tell. There wasn't much of a threat. The creators already knew where we were. Michael running back to them wouldn't change that. The only thing that had been hurt was my heart. Because with Michael gone, any hope of him returning to me had been destroyed.

I felt hot tears start to slide down my face, although it remained expressionless. My feet stumbled across the clearing, my mind repeating one word over and over again in my mind like a broken record. *Michael.*

I reached Marian's tent minutes later and found her reading on her bed. I didn't know why I had wanted her. I didn't know why she was the first person I wanted to tell. Maybe because she was so understanding, so kind. She wouldn't pity me like Beatrix or Cassandra, and she wouldn't freak out like Jessica. She would just comfort me, and I didn't care if it was selfish to want to tell her first instead of Jessica.

Marian stood up abruptly. "Drew," she said, her voice laced with concern. "What's wrong?"

I stood there, tears streaming down my face, not trying to hold them back because I knew it was no use. "Michael," I heard myself saying, although the voice coming out sounded nothing like mine. "He's gone."

Marian's expression softened. "He escaped?" she asked.

I nodded. I opened my mouth to say more, to reassure her he couldn't affect our plan, to tell her how much this hurt, but I faltered. Before I could say a word, Marian had crossed the space between us and enveloped me in a hug. I cried into her shoulder until my tears ran dry.

* * * *

I was back by the cells, staring at the empty room in which Michael had stayed for so long. I hadn't touched the door; I hadn't touched anything. The room was silent. I could hear my breathing; steady and consistent. My eyes watered from being held open too long, and I blinked, clearing my vision.

I stood up from my chair and made my way to the cell. I reached out to touch the door, strangely feeling closer to Michael, knowing he was the last person to touch it this way. I told myself I was silly and let go, my fingers sliding slowly off the metal.

I walked into the cell, trying to imagine what it must have felt like to live here for so long; bars keeping you back from life. Tears sprang to my eyes again. *You're better off out of here,* I thought. I reached up to wipe my eyes, but I glanced something in the corner. Something on the floor.

I walked closer to get a better look, and what I saw made my eyes widen. All those weeks of Michael scratching away at the stone floor. What had he been doing? The answer stared me in the eyes as I looked down to see my face etched in the stone.

My eyes were open and staring, my mouth curved downward like it normally does when I have no smile or frown to express. I was expressionless, simply watching. Like I had done for so many weeks.

I frowned, realizing I had never known Michael could draw. He had never told me. It almost scared me how lifelike the drawing was. Her eyes drew me in, and I could almost tell that they were blue.

I stood there, staring into my eyes until the Stone Drew drove me away with her expressionless gaze.

Chapter Twenty-seven

We need a way to get into the Institution, the paper read. That phrase had been repeating in my mind for days now. We needed a plan, but what? We had used multiple ways before, but by now, I knew the creators must have stepped up the Institution security. Yvonne quickly saw my words and looked up at me, shrugging. I held in a groan of frustration; not so much with her, but with the situation. *We can't use tactics we've used before,* I wrote. *Ideas?*

Yvonne frowned, her forehead wrinkling in thought. I thought as well, although my brain was all thought out. I had gone over plan after plan, realizing none of them would work. I needed someone who knew the Institution and the creators inside and out. I needed Yvonne.

Suddenly she looked up, a smile covering her face. She grabbed the pen and paper, furiously scribbling. *Jeremy,* the paper said. Jeremy. Hundreds of memories flooded my mind. Memories of Jeremy back at the Institution, memories of our days with Yvonne and him, breaking into the Institution.

I looked down at the paper and smiled.

* * * *

We had a plan. Not a great plan, but a pretty good one. A plan rushed together, but well thought out at the same time. A plan we hoped and prayed would work.

Jeremy was the inside man, Yvonne was the hacker and Cassandra, Beatrix, Cameron, and I were the guards. We didn't dare bring any others for fear of being caught. This was a large job that needed only a few people.

Yvonne had found a way to contact Jeremy through text, going through various questions and answers to prove that it was really him. Jeremy had agreed to play a prerecorded tape of an empty hallway over the camera recording screen, making our entrance clean and unnoticeable. A quick meeting with him in a private setting got us a key to unlock the doors without an alarm sounding. If the plan went smoothly, we would get in, guard Yvonne while she hacked the computers, and get out. It seemed like the perfectly thought out plan. If it went smoothly...

Which they never seemed to do.

It was perfect. Almost too perfect. But we didn't have time to redesign our plan. We didn't have time for plan B in case of problems or timing. We didn't have time to wait another day.

We were leaving in the morning. Leaving to save the perfected, or become one once again.

Chapter Twenty-eight

It was dark. One o'clock in the morning. The car rattled as we bounced along the pothole-filled road. We were quiet, listening to our breathing and the beating of our hearts. No one said a word. No one had anything to say. I looked out the window, but all I saw was black.

Cassandra leaned forward from the back seat to hand me a small, cheap, pre-paid cell phone. She quickly handed one to everyone else. "Just in case we get separated. We'll text each other alerts," she reminded us in a barely audible whisper – Yvonne was still equipped with the creators' recording device. This would be her last chance to explain things. Possibly her last time explaining anything if we didn't play this right. She just didn't say it out loud. Saying it out loud seemed to make it more real. She glanced around at all of us to make sure we had all heard it; she had whispered it so quietly on account of Yvonne's recording chip.

I took one last glance around the car. Cassandra, Cameron, and Yvonne were all sitting in the back seat, Yvonne in the middle, and Beatrix was driving the car. They all looked scared; their faces were white. Something flipped in my stomach, and I tried to calm my nerves.

Suddenly the car came to a stop, and once Beatrix shut off the engine, it was deadly silent. I couldn't even hear breathing. We sat there for a moment, just sitting. I finally motioned for everyone to get going, and we all quickly left the vehicle.

Beatrix had parked the car in an old grocery store parking lot a few blocks away from the Institution, and the plan was to return here after our sabotage. I gave everyone one last nervous look. We were all wearing black; black shirts, jeans, and sneakers.

How original.

My hair was pulled tight into a ponytail, out of my eyes, and my face felt oddly exposed; the searing wind of early winter stung my face. I clutched the gun in my hand, wishing we didn't need to have them, but knowing that they would be good backup as a last resort. I saw a flash of light and looked over to see that Yvonne had just received a text message. After a quick glance at her phone, she turned to us and showed us the text saying that the recording was in place.

We trudged through the few inches of snow that covered the ground, and I looked up, upon feeling something cold and wet brush against my skin, to see that it was snowing. I stared up at the polka-dotted sky and watched as the snow slowly fluttered to the ground.

We were walking faster now, hurrying down the sidewalk, getting closer and closer to the Institution. We were all silent; all we could hear was the quiet padding of our footsteps against the snow and the quiet scraping noise as our arms brushed against our sides.

When the Institution came into view, my first instinct was to halt, but I forced my legs onward toward the back door we had been instructed to enter through. I swiped the card key and watched as the little light turned from red to green, and the door unlocked. I shot a smile at the others, and we slipped into the dark hallway.

There were no noises, just the hum of the dim lights overhead and the tension in the air. Jeremy had told us about all the guard posts, and we hurried down the hallway, being sure to avoid them. I knew where the computer room was, as I had been there before, but Yvonne led the way down the corridor. She knew this place better than I did. It seemed like a lifetime ago since I had been here.

The hallway widened, and doors came more frequently. My heart was pounding in my chest and I kept my breathing low. The hand that was holding my gun was beginning to sweat, and I had to change hands frequently, careful to avoid the trigger. Our footsteps suddenly seemed too loud, and I waved my hands, motioning for us to slow down. We tiptoed across the floor and finally reached the door to the computer room. Yvonne slowed down and held a finger up to her lips, jerking her head in the direction of the door.

Flawed

There was someone inside. There was always someone inside. We neatly lined up beside the door, and on the count of three, Yvonne yanked it open. We all rushed in, and the creator at the desk turned sharply around, his eyes wide with shock. He reached for something at his belt; a gun. But Cameron already had his pistol pointed at the creator's forehead. "Don't move." His voice was low, and his eyes were dark and menacing. The creator drew in a shaky breath and raised his hands slightly higher. Cassandra quickly headed toward the man and, finding him still human, quickly knocked him out with a hit to the back of his neck. The creator crumpled in his chair, and Beatrix and I hurriedly moved him to the floor.

Yvonne quickly took the seat and immediately started typing away at the computer. I watched as box after box popped up on the screen, and multiple warning noises accompanied by red lettering flashed across the monitor.

I jogged to the door and quickly looked out into the hallway. I saw no signs of creators or androids, but I waved Cameron and Cassandra over anyway. "*You* stay right outside the door, and *you* watch from down the hallway," I told Cassandra and then Cameron. They nodded and Cameron sprinted down the corridor as Cassandra stationed herself by the entrance. I partially shut the door and headed back to where Yvonne was busy typing away, Beatrix at her side.

"I thought you said you could do this," I whispered to her, noticing the she had gotten no farther.

Yvonne turned to glare daggers at me. "It's not a piece of cake, you know," she snapped and then pointed to her neck and widened her eyes, reminding me of our constant watch. I shut my mouth and started to pace back and forth.

Seconds ticked by, and my heart sped up. It seemed with every minute that passed my breathing and heart rate increased in speed. Multiple times I thought I heard footsteps, only to find that it was Beatrix shifting in the hallway.

I rubbed my hands together and tightened my ponytail. Two minutes. Three minutes. Four minutes. Five minutes.

I heard a clinking noise and turned to look at the computer. Yvonne was in.

Suddenly all three of our phones flashed, and I looked around in confusion. We hadn't planned any updates during this time. Something had to be wrong. I pulled out my phone and read the message. My eyes widened. Caught...

Suddenly the door burst open, and my eyes flew to Cassandra standing in the doorway. "They're coming," she hissed, her normally light eyes shadowed by darkness and filled with dread.

Yvonne turned around, seeming to be the calmest out of all of us, but still the crankiest. "I need more time," she hissed back, her tone threatening to break into hysteria. I looked frantically from Cassandra to Yvonne.

Cassandra shook her head again. "They're coming *now*."

Yvonne cursed and turned back to the computer. I ran to the doorway and looked out. Cameron was running at full speed toward us, shaking his head, and waving behind him. I saw no creators or androids at the moment, but I knew they must be close. Suddenly I heard footsteps thundering our way, and I knew our time was up. "Yvonne," I snapped.

"Not done," she hissed back.

I clenched my fists and let out a frustrated sigh. "Doesn't matter, we're leaving."

"I'm so close," she replied.

"Yvonne!" I nearly shrieked, watching as the androids came into view. I heard her hurry up behind me with another string of profanity, and we were all out in the hallway and running. I quickly checked to make sure that everyone had made it out, and we sprinted down the corridor.

I could hear shouts and footsteps behind us, and I realized I had no idea where this hallway ended or led to. I had never spent much time in this section of the Institution. Androids were rarely allowed here.

"End of the hallway, turn right. Then there's a window," Yvonne told us, as if reading my mind. I nodded gratefully, and she took the lead. Halfway there, though, I knew we weren't going to make it. The androids were gaining, and we were falling behind. I could almost feel them breathing on my neck, reaching out to grab me. I heard a yell as Cassandra's arm was grasped, and she was yanked to a halt. I stopped and turned, ready to fight, but suddenly I heard a gunshot and the android holding Cassandra let go to tend to the bullet now embedded in his foot. I raised my gun and pointed it at them, freezing them to their spots. There were only five androids, not a lot, and they didn't have weapons. Beatrix, Cassandra, Cameron, and Yvonne shuffled behind me, and I could see the window out of the corner of my eyes. I opened my mouth to explain instructions, but something made my words collapse and die on the tip of my tongue. My mouth dropped open as I looked to see a mass of androids at the end of the hallway swarming our way. They would catch us. There was no way for us to get away; not with that many androids. But suddenly a thought flew to my mind. The memory of the androids at the parking lot. My mind was racing, my heart hammering, and thoughts were swarming through my brain, but only one made sense. I turned to the others. "Go!" I yelled. Cassandra opened her mouth in shock and shook her head. I pointed to the window, my gun still raised at the androids. "You said I'm in charge, and I'm telling you to go," I screamed at them, willing them to turn and leave me. They all hesitated, but only for a split second before Cameron, Cassandra, and Beatrix were sprinting down the hallway. Out of the corner of my eye I saw the androids getting closer. I stared Yvonne in the eyes as if daring her to question me. "You, too, Yvonne." My voice was low and cold. "Go." She took one last look at me with her dark, beautiful eyes, and then she was gone.

I faced the androids coming my way and backed up toward the wall. They joined the original five and then stopped. It seemed as if I should have felt something; relief, surprise, confusion? But I didn't. I knew they would leave the others. I knew they would want me first.

Just like they had in the parking lot.

Although, I didn't know why.

The androids stared at me; at least fifteen of them, the various shades of eyes, all seeming blank and colorless.

But just then I saw someone at the edge of the crowd—long blonde hair and bright blue eyes. Eerily blue eyes. She caught my gaze and held it for a few seconds. Suddenly I recognized her as the woman I'd met outside the hotel, though by now it seemed like such a long time ago. And now that I fell deeper into her blue-eyed gaze, I realized she had been the one to drop the key in my cell. I opened my mouth in confusion, ready to call out to her, but before I could utter a word, she turned and disappeared around the corner. I took a step forward, nearly forgetting about all the androids surrounding me. For some reason, I couldn't let her go.

Suddenly, I saw a creator emerge from the crowd; tall, gray-eyed, and angry. My expression hardened into a glare, and I held my gun more firmly as I stared into Glen's eyes, the woman forgotten.

"Drew," he said. He had said my name before like this. Not a greeting, not a question. Just a statement. He shook his head as if feeling sorry about something.

I pointed the gun at his head. He stared back at me evenly. "You thought you could get away with it," he said quietly.

Anger boiled up inside of me.

"You should have known you never could beat us." His tone wasn't mocking or angry, just monotone.

I stood still, my gun pointed at him, watching.

Glen stood there for a moment, as if thinking out his next move. He turned to face the crowd of androids. "Leave," he ordered. "I want to talk with Drew." His voice was commanding yet relaxed. Immediately the androids turned and filed away; all except two, who stayed fixed by Glen's side.

I noticed none of them had guns, and I prayed he hadn't sent anyone to get some. But then I realized how silly that prayer was. Glen was just playing with me. I wouldn't get out of here. I had known that when I had told the others to leave.

"The tape never played," Glen said, his eyes dancing with delight. "Your plan was obvious, really," he said with a laugh. A laugh that was high-pitched and made my skin crawl.

"Why do you want to talk with me?" I heard myself saying. My voice was much more timid and afraid than I had intended it to be, but I fixed that with a harsh stare.

Glen shrugged, as if it were unimportant. "You know what we're going to do with you, don't you?" he asked.

I narrowed my eyes. *Stop playing with me!* I wanted to scream.

Glen shook his head. "It's actually very sad," he said, his expression one of mock concern. "I wish we didn't have to do this, but you know

Drew, you did choose this for yourself." His words were playful and so were his eyes.

Suddenly, my anger seemed to well up so high I couldn't hold it in anymore. "Chose what?" I nearly screamed, suddenly too aware of the gun in my hands, which was itching to be shot. "I chose *nothing*! I never wanted to be like this."

Glen's expression morphed into one of understanding. He smiled slightly. "You're right. You didn't choose to become perfect. *I* chose that for you." His tone was mocking.

"I'm not perfect," I spat, tears starting to well up in my eyes. Angry and surprised, I furiously blinked them away.

"Oh, but you are, Drew. Do you think I'd risk *you* if I wasn't sure?" Glen's voice was almost normal now. Almost kind, almost human.

I turned my head and stared at him in confusion. My eyes narrowed in suspicion. "What do you mean?" I asked slowly. I watched carefully at the way his eyes widened slightly and a smile tugged at the corners of his mouth.

"You mean you haven't figured it out by now?" he asked, his voice threatening to break into a laugh.

I glowered at him. "What?" I spat, my teeth clenched.

Glen's face became serious again, and he looked at me for such a long moment I thought that maybe he had forgotten what he was about to say. "That you were the first, Drew," he said evenly. His lips spread into a smile. "My first success."

I stood there, silent, unmoving, staring at him. "The first android?" I repeated. "I was the first android?" My voice sounded hollow as it echoed throughout the corridor.

Glen nodded, his eyes shining.

My heart was beating faster. Thousands of thoughts swirled through my mind. If I was the first, did that change anything? "I was still human, though?" I heard myself blurt out. "I'm not a complete machine?" I couldn't help but detect the hint of desperation lining my voice.

"No, you're not a complete machine. You were human once. Just as human as *I* was." He stared intently into my eyes, his gaze pinning me to the wall.

My mind was whirling. "Then how come I don't remember anything from before I was an android?" I couldn't help but ask. I needed to know. I didn't care of if I was going to die today, I needed to know. "You know how the flaweds' minds work. They remember."

Glen's smile widened, and he suppressed a laugh. He held out his hands in an explaining gesture. "But you do, Drew," he said quietly. "All those years growing up with Yvonne, don't you remember that?"

I frowned, opening my mouth, but pausing before replying. "But, I was an android." My voice was defensive and disbelieving. All those years, all those memories – they couldn't be real.

Glen closed his eyes and shook his head, shifted his feet, and then turned back to me. "You weren't perfected until you were fifteen," he said frankly. "You can't perfect a child. They're still growing. It wouldn't work." He talked as if he were explaining his profession to anyone. The way I had heard him talk countless times.

I stared at him, completely confused and dumbfounded. He had waited until I was fifteen before he perfected me. "Then why was I…" Pieces began to fit together in my mind.

Glen's smile didn't falter. He just watched me with his cold, gray eyes, telling me something his words couldn't quite do justice. Telling me something only Glen could tell.

My mouth dropped open, and the gun fell to my side. I wanted to look away. I didn't want to stare into the face of a man I hated even more than I already had, but somehow I couldn't tear my gaze away.

"People thought you were crazy," I started to say quietly, remembering all the things the creators had drilled me on; about how special we were, about how nobody had thought we could make it, but we had. "You wanted to test your idea." My voice was wavering, and fear gripped my chest.

Glen was expressionless.

"So you tested it on your daughter." My voice was a whisper, a thought, a reality. I stared into Glen's eyes, and we stood there, motionless, for what seemed like decades, but it was only a few minutes. I remembered all the times as a little girl when Glen had told me how special I was, how I was an android built for amazing things, but he never once mentioned that I was his daughter. He must have always known what he would do with me.

"And it worked," Glen's voice reached out to me, full of pride and satisfaction. A sick satisfaction, one filled with evil and power.

Anger welled up inside of me, and I wanted to scream. "Then why did you shut me off?" I asked, my voice rising. There were so many things I wanted to scream at him, but I forced myself to stay calm.

Glen bit his lip as if deciding what to tell me. "We didn't," he said calmly. "Your body went into shock during the operation."

My legs suddenly felt wobbly, and my head was starting to spin.

Glen rubbed his hand against his head and went on. "On top of that, some idiot let your oxygen supply run low, and you fell into a coma." He was watching me closely now, as if wondering how well this was going over. "But you eventually came out," he added. "And we used that story to cover it up."

"And what about Yvonne? Did you mess up on her, too?" My voice was accusatory, and I glared at him, my words dripping with malice.

Glen shook his head, ignoring my stare. "She was the second, and also the daughter of a fellow colleague, but no, everything went well for her."

I stood there, staring at him for a moment, wondering how a man so evil, so selfish, so inhumane, could be my father.

"And what about my mom?" I finally asked. "Was she just as sick as you?"

Glen's eyes flashed angrily, but he quickly regained his composure. "She agreed with me at first, and although she's since had her doubts, I've convinced her of the right choice."

I stared at him for a long moment. "Convinced her?" I echo.

He nodded, his expression hardening, and I knew that although I could see in his eyes that he must have threatened her, forced her to agree, he wasn't going to say it out loud. "She agrees with me now," he said slowly.

"She's here," I said quietly. Glen nodded, and I felt anger burning up inside of me. Anger that I'd wished for a family all my life, only to find that they were right here all along. Only this family was twisted and cruel.

"Instead of sacrificing your life, you sacrificed mine," I said quietly, although fire burned in my eyes.

Glen's smile dropped from his face. "I made you perfect." His voice hardened. "I made you what you are."

"Stop calling me that!" I screamed at him, tears dripping down my face, although from what I wasn't even sure. Something inside of me snapped, and I felt my hands clench at my sides. "Don't you see what you did to me?" The gun seemed unsteady in my hands, ready to go off at any minute, and for a second, I didn't trust myself with it. "I spent my whole life trying to be perfect like you said I was, when deep down I knew I wasn't! I thought there was something wrong with *me*." A laugh came out of my throat; dry and almost like a sob. My body started shaking. "I never thought I was good enough. I was never good enough for you. I was trying to live up to something I could never be!"

Glen took a step toward me, but I raised the gun and glared at him. "Why would you do this to me?" I ran a hand over my face, wiping the tears away. "Why would you even tell me this? Just to make me feel worse about myself? At least before, I could daydream about the family I'd had. About the family who could have actually loved me. Not the one who turned me into a *monster*." I was shaking uncontrollably now, sobs emerging from my throat. I tried to stop. I tried to stop and remain in control. I couldn't let Glen have this effect on me. But everything was crashing down on me all at once. Everything was crushing me, and all I could think to do was cry.

"Drew, you should be grateful for what I did for you," Glen snapped at me.

I focused on him through the veil of tears, and I felt my face form into a grimace. I held the gun up and pointed it at his head. *Shoot,* something told me. "Don't." My voice was wavering. I cocked the gun.

Glen remained expressionless. "You were nothing before I made you what you are," he spat, digging my wound deeper.

I glared at him through the tears. "I hate you." My voice was choked by sobs. My fingers shook above the trigger. I stared into his eyes. *Shoot.*

Everything hurt. My head ached; my heart ached. I was fighting some unspoken battle. A battle between my desires and my conscience. Tears streamed down my face, and I heard another sob escape my throat. I squeezed my eyes shut, and my heart seemed to freeze. I couldn't kill Glen. I shifted the gun and pointed at his leg.

Flawed

I pulled the trigger.

Chapter Twenty-nine

I forgot about the two androids stationed by Glen. I hadn't noticed them slowly inching my way during our conversation. I hadn't noticed until too late how they leaped at me as I pulled the trigger. I felt one of the androids collide into me, and the kick of the pistol sent it flying behind me. I fell to the ground and heard Glen shout out something unintelligible.

The android sat on top of me, pinning me to the ground, and I looked over to see Glen standing up from where he had fallen. I saw the rip in his pant leg and realized I hadn't hit him square on, but only grazed his thigh. But by the amount of blood staining his jeans I suspected it had grazed him badly.

I was pulled roughly to my feet to meet Glen's menacing stare. "You're dead," he spat at me. "You've been ready to be replaced for a long time." He motioned for the androids to follow him, and we all went walking down the hallway. I struggled against the android that was holding me, but that only made his grip tighter, so I stopped.

Glen led us to a doorway and motioned for the two androids to wait outside. I glared at him suspiciously, but he pulled me inside anyway. The room was dark until Glen switched the bright light on, causing me to blink and shade my eyes.

When I finally adjusted to the brightness, I looked around to see a room full of tubes and laboratory equipment. I frowned in confusion, and I turned to look at Glen. He was watching me with a sick, delighted smile on his face, an expression I had never seen. It frightened me, and I took a step away from him and toward the tables littered with tools. My eyes glanced at the words written on the labels, and I stopped, my heart ceasing to beat.

DREW. The labels read in capital, bold letters. I frowned and leaned closer to take another look. DNA samples, photos, and long lists of information covered the tabletops. Suddenly, my mind flashed back to the day in the parking lot where the androids had wanted me and not Beatrix. I turned slowly to look back at Glen, my mouth open to say something, but no words seemed to fit.

Glen tilted his head and smiled. "Why are you so special?" he asked, as if reading my thoughts, saying the words I was too afraid to say myself.

I wanted to tell him to stop. To stop bombarding me with more than I had ever wanted to know. I wanted to ask him why he was doing this if he was just going to kill me anyway, but something inside of me screamed to know the answer.

"What is this?" My voice was trembling, because deep down, something inside of me was terrified of finding out that I might have come from one of these tubes.

"Ah, Drew." His tone was completely different from how it had been a moment ago. It was the tone he had used with me before I had betrayed him. The hardness of his voice was gone and replaced by a proud tone I had rarely heard. I noticed he wasn't staring into my eyes, but gazing into the distance behind me. I frowned.

Glen's eyes suddenly darted back to mine, and his expression changed. "You're special because you need to be replaced," he said evenly, his gray eyes as cold as sleet.

My heart wasn't beating, my lungs weren't working, and my limbs had lost their feeling as I slowly turned around to stare into the deep blue eyes of a girl I had known all my life.

Drew.

Chapter Thirty

Drew stared back at me, her eyes expressionless. I couldn't move. I couldn't do anything except stare at her. Stare at me.

"I had such great plans for you Drew," Glen's voice called from behind me. "You were to rule the new world alongside me." I heard him making a 'tsk' sound and clicking his tongue. "Too bad you chose to leave all that behind."

My breathing had come back, and it was starting to increase in speed. I was almost hyperventilating, and I tried to calm myself down. I stared into Drew's eyes, but for some reason, I couldn't quite find what I was looking for. Drew's eyes were blank, focusing on mine, but still empty and careless.

What was she? My mind raced back to the day at school when I had spent hours staring into my eyes to find a soul hidden somewhere beneath the blue. I hadn't seen what I now knew was there because I hadn't expected it to be there in the first place. But whenever I had looked into someone's eyes, Jessica's, Michael's, even Yvonne's … something had always been there. And even now, when I looked at myself, I saw who I was.

But when I stared into this Drew's eyes there was nothing. Nothing at all. Just a glossy blue.

I slowly turned back to Glen. "What … is she…?" My voice was barely a whisper.

A smile spread slowly across Glen's face, distorting his features into something terrible and sickly. "She's perfect," he replied. "*Really* perfect. Incapable of flaws. This time I made a truly perfect android."

I opened my mouth, but no words came. I looked back at the robot Drew, knowing there was no human hiding beneath her perfect features. "She's not real," I whispered, not taking my eyes off of her.

"But she is," Glen protested. "She's more my daughter than you ever were."

My breath caught in my throat, although I wasn't even facing Glen. Those words hit me like a slap in the face even though I had only now realized the truth beneath our relationship. The father I had always imagined was kind and loving, not this monster standing behind me. "So what are you going to do now?" I asked quietly, although I knew the answer. I had known the answer since the day I had decided to first go against Glen's rules. Deep down I knew he would never stand for this betrayal. Not without getting his payback.

"You know the answer to that," he replied, his voice strangely expressionless. "We can't have *two* Drews."

My heart seemed to stop beating at the sound of those words; my blood freezing to ice in my veins, and my mind denying the idea that those words could be true. They sounded more terrible than I had ever imagined them sounding. Evil, inhumane, and sickening.

Glen grabbed my arm from behind me and pulled me toward the door. I didn't struggle or even say a word. I knew it was no use. Before I left, I took one last look into the robot Drew's eyes. They sparkled as she slowly opened her mouth to speak.

"Goodbye, Drew," she said.

Chapter Thirty-one

Her voice had sounded like mine. Her eyes had looked like mine. But at the same time she was nothing like me. Her voice had been monotone, and her eyes were strangely blank.

I let Glen pull me along down the hallway until we entered the familiar setting of the lobby. I let him lead me down the hallway and through a door to the right. With a sickening realization, I recognized this room to be the place where I had seen the boy so long ago. The unconscious boy lying on an operating table.

My heart was pounding, and I clenched my fists. Glen locked the door to the hallway and walked over to the counter at the far end of the room. I heard a click and looked up to see two androids enter the room from another doorway. They stationed themselves around the room, watching me closely, and with a jolt I recognized one of them as Michael.

I opened my mouth to say his name, but the word disintegrated at the tip of my tongue. Why try? After all those months, why try again now?

His expression showed recognition, but not the kind I was looking for. He recognized me as the girl who had held him captive for so long, not the girl he had once loved. Tears sprang to my eyes, but I refused to cry. Not anymore. Never again. I knew I only had minutes to live, and I didn't want to spend them feeling sorry for myself.

Glen jerked his head in my direction, and Michael and the other android walked over to me. My first reflex was to back away, but they firmly grabbed my arms and pulled me over to the table. I struggled, but only halfheartedly.

"Michael," I said, in one last plea for him to remember, but he didn't respond. He only picked me up and hoisted me onto the table while I kicked and squirmed, the other android holding down my arms.

They had a firm grip on either side of me, pinning me to the table. Out of the corner of my eye I saw Glen adjusting something into a small syringe. My heart was racing. I was on the verge of crying, but I tried as hard as I could to hold it back. *Calm down, Drew,* I told myself. *It's okay...*

I closed my eyes and thought about God. I thought about all the times I had prayed. I thought about everything I had done. I thought about my actions, and I hoped they were good enough. I thought about shooting Glen in the leg, and the hatred I had harbored no longer felt so strong. I felt a tear slide out of the corner of my eye. *Forgive me.* Another tear escaped.

My eyes opened to see Glen coming my way. I didn't look at the needle. I didn't want to. I didn't want to break the fleeting moment of serenity I had.

"It's just an overdose of pain medication," Glen's voice said quietly. "You won't feel anything."

Was that sorrow I heard in his voice? It couldn't be. Glen wasn't the type.

I turned my head in the other direction and looked at Michael. I stared into his dark brown eyes, and I smiled slightly. He stared back at me, a puzzled expression painting his face; watching.

I closed my eyes, no longer wanting to see anymore. No longer wanting to see Michael's face indifferent and no longer wanting to see Glen stare at me with the hatred I knew he felt. I was done. Right as my eyelids slid shut I thought I saw a word form on Michael's lips. I thought he had just mouthed something to me. I thought he had just said, "Drew."

Just then I felt the needle slide into my skin, and I held in a gasp. A gasp of horror, shock, and fear.

Take me home.

Chapter Thirty-two

The needle stung as is slid under my skin. I heard a noise, although I couldn't tell what it was. A hand that had been holding me down released me, and I heard Glen's voice; strained, angry, frantic. I felt the needle being quickly removed from my skin, and I wondered how many seconds I had to live.

I felt arms slide under my back and knees, lifting me from the table. I vaguely wondered what was going on, but realized I couldn't open my eyes. I tried to make a noise, but my mouth didn't seem to be working either. My arms and legs were tingling and my breathing was slow. My head fell to the side against something firm and solid and I felt myself being jostled around as I was being carried.

I heard a voice, deep and worried. It said my name a few times, and I could hear his breathing in my ear as he carried me along. *Michael?* I thought vaguely. My ears told me it was so, but my mind refused to believe it. My reasoning told me that Michael no longer remembered me, no longer loved me.

But that voice had sounded a lot like him.

My mind was wandering. Where was I? Why wasn't I dead? I wondered, vaguely, if I was dying. Everything was so hazy.

I rested my head against his shoulder as my mind slowly lost its reasoning, understanding, and consciousness; as the drug took over and my mind went blank.

The last thing I remember was the beating of Michael's heart.

* * * *

It was quiet. There was a small rustling noise that made me wonder where I was. Slowly, feeling was beginning to come back to my arms and legs. My head throbbed, and I felt nauseous. There was tingling in my toes and the tips of my fingers. I heard another noise and then a voice. It said my name, but I couldn't open my eyes. It was the same voice. The same voice I had thought was Michael's. Was it really him? My heart leaped, wanting to believe it.

I felt something touch my shoulders and then fingers brush against my forehead. My eyes hurt, but I forced them open.

"Drew!" the voice said again, and this time, I was sure it was Michael's. I wanted to leap up and throw my arms around his neck, but everything hurt so badly I could barely manage to open my mouth and reply. "Michael," I said, a smile slowly starting to creep into my expression. His lips formed into a smile I hadn't seen on him in what seemed like years.

I had almost forgotten how beautiful his smile was. The way the corners of his mouth looked like they might dimple, but they didn't fully, and the way his nose crinkled slightly when he laughed.

I realized I was partially sitting up and leaning against Michael. I looked around to see trees in every direction and snow covering the ground. The morning sun was beginning to rise, sending yellow and pink streaks of light through the trees.

I was smiling so wide I thought I might never stop, and I didn't care if everything hurt. I sat up straighter, leaned toward Michael, and pressed my lips against his. He immediately kissed me back and I hadn't realized how much I had missed this, how much I had missed *him*, until that moment. My arms found their way around his neck, and I was hugging him so tightly I was almost surprised he could breathe. His arms wrapped around me as well and hugged me back.

All those months of devastation, waiting and hoping for Michael to come back to me, seemed so far away. Here I was, in his arms, and never had I felt safer; more at home.

Eventually we broke away, and I leaned my head against his shoulder, his arms still wrapped firmly around me. We sat there, holding on to each other and just listening to our breathing and beating hearts until the tingling left my limbs and my strength returned.

Michael helped me to my feet and I found that I was still a little unsteady. "I don't know how much of that stuff got into your system," Michael told me. "I pulled it out pretty fast, but you still got way more than you ever should. I tried to get you out quickly, but Glen and that other android made things a little harder."

Nothing he could say would make my smile disappear so I merely grinned at him. He smiled back for a moment and then his smile faded. I gave him a questioning look.

He frowned, and he looked down at his feet. "I'm sorry, Drew," he said quietly. "All those days you sat there..." he trailed off, and I took a step closer to him.

I shook my head. "It's not your fault," I said.

There was a pause. "I thought you were dead," he said finally. "You were out for a while. I thought that I hadn't gotten the needle out in time." There was pain in his eyes, and I wanted nothing more than that pain to be gone.

"Michael," I said firmly. "You saved my life. You're back, and I'm alive." I smiled at him and watched the light slowly return to his eyes. We stood there for a moment before I broke the silence. "Wait, how did you get out?" I asked, realizing that there must have been guards or creators.

Michael shrugged. "There was a woman in the lobby. At first, I thought she was a creator, but she just disabled the alarm and let me through the door." He seemed just as confused as I was about the circumstances until a thought dawned on me.

"We need to find the others," I declared, and Michael nodded.

"Should we go back to the flawed camp?" he asked.

I thought for a moment, wondering if the creators had already gone there, but then I nodded. "We need to see who's there," I told him.

Michael clarified exactly where we were, and I decided we should start walking in the direction of the camp. We trudged through the deep snow and found our way to the road.

"I didn't know you could draw," I said quietly as we walked, remembering the drawing on the stone floor of Michael's cell.

Michael was silent for a moment before he nodded. "I don't do it much," he finally said. "Once in a while." He turned to look at me. "You saw the picture?"

I nodded, still watching him. There was a pause. "Why'd you draw it?" I asked.

It took Michael a moment to reply and when he did he seemed unsure, as if he didn't even know himself. "I knew I was supposed to remember you. Something told me that I knew you, but I didn't know how and I didn't want to believe it," he added. I was quiet, waiting for him to go on. He shrugged. "I don't know why I drew it, I just wanted to." He turned to look at me again, his expression telling me more than his words ever could. "You seemed important to me, but I didn't know why."

I looked back at him, my expression melting into a small smile.

We walked for about five minutes before I broke the silence. The realization had been haunting my mind for a while, and I needed to share it. "Glen's my father," I said quietly and Michael turned to look at me in shock.

"He's your *what*?" he asked, looking completely dumbfounded.

I nodded. "I was the first person he tested it on—the whole android thing. I was the first," I explained, watching the ground we were walking on.

"But…" Michael trailed off.

"I don't know what to think," I told him truthfully. "I want to hate him but at the same time I don't."

Michael still looked surprised, and I almost dreaded to tell him what I was about to say. But someone besides me needed to know, or I would burst.

"And since I betrayed him by running away," I said, then paused a few seconds, "he created a new me."

Michael stopped walking, and I was forced to stop with him. "A new you?" he echoed, as if uncertain about whether he had heard it right.

I nodded slowly. "She's not real," I said, thinking back to the Institution when I had stared into her blank, lifeless eyes. "She's a genuine android. She's a real machine." I wasn't looking at Michael. I was staring off into the trees, reliving the scene in my mind, including the pain and horror I had felt upon this realization.

"We'll stop him," Michael said firmly. "He's done with being 'king' and 'creator'."

I nodded absentmindedly and we continued on our way.

* * * *

It took us about two hours to reach the flawed camp, and by then, it was still only mid morning. When it first came into view, I felt a surge of excitement, but then immediately realized that something was wrong.

Michael and I walked cautiously into the clearing, looking around at the deserted tents and buildings. "Where are they?" I asked quietly. A few tents lay sideways and bent, and there was no sign of anyone around.

"The creators," Michael replied. "They got here first."

I stared around at the deserted area, thinking of the people we had left behind when we had set out on our mission; Jessica, Marian, and dozens of other names and faces I had grown accustomed to over the past months.

Suddenly I remembered my cell phone, and it felt hot in my pocket at the realization. I reached in to grab it quickly and punched in the number to the cell phone that had been given to Jessica. I prayed she still had it with her and that she hadn't been abducted by the creators. I listened as the phone rang once, twice, five times, and then Jessica answered, her voice scratchy.

"Jessica?" I asked quickly, gripping the phone to my ear.

"Drew!" I heard her exclaim. "Are you okay, where are you?" she asked frantically. "We got attacked!"

"I'm fine," I replied, looking over to see Michael watching me and my phone conversation. I smiled. "I've got good news."

"Good news? At a time like this?" Jessica asked incredulously. "Well, don't go back to the camp, the creators were there," she added quickly. "We spotted them before they reached us, and we managed to get away just as they were coming. We're about five miles away from camp, out in the woods."

"We're already at camp," I replied. "But we can probably find you."

"You're with the others?" she asked.

"No, we got separated," I explained. "I had hoped they had gone to find you."

I heard Jessica make a clicking sound with her tongue. "No, they haven't come back."

"We'll try to find you," I answered. "You said five miles? In which direction?" I asked her.

"The opposite direction of the road," Jessica replied with a laugh. "Couldn't tell you the real direction for the life of me. Oh, and who's *we*?"

Her voice paused on the line, and I waited for a moment, staring at Michael with a smile. I laughed softly. "Michael." There was dead silence over the phone, and for a moment, I thought we had been disconnected. "Jessica?"

"Is he…?" Her voice was quiet.

"Yes," I replied, nodding at the same time, although I knew she couldn't see me. "He's himself again, and he's standing right here."

I heard something that sounded like a sigh and a sob from the other end of the line and then I heard Jessica laughing. "Can I talk to him?" she asked, her voice overflowing with excitement and joy.

I smiled and handed the phone to her brother.

"Michael!" Jessica shrieked so loudly I could hear it from where I was standing. Michael laughed his smile widening. I watched them talk for awhile, all the time a grin etched on Michael's face. After a few moments, they ended their call, and we started on our way to find the flawed.

I took my cell phone back and dialed Beatrix's number, hoping that she'd answer. She picked up the phone immediately, and her voice sounded desperate. "Drew?" she asked breathlessly.

"Yeah," I replied. "Where are you guys, are you okay?"

"We're fine, how are *you*?" Her voice sounded close to panic, and I wondered how much time she had spent worrying.

"I'm fine, believe me," I said with a smile, casting a sidelong glance at Michael.

"We've been worried sick about you," she answered, sounding relieved. "Where are you?"

"We're at the flawed camp, but they evacuated," I explained. I quickly relayed the crude directions Jessica had given me, and Beatrix promised they'd meet us there.

"Who are you with?" she asked quizzically. "You implied someone was with you."

I couldn't hold back my grin. "Michael," I replied, and I saw him turn my way with a smile. I could hear Beatrix's shock over the phone as she sputtered for an explanation. I laughed. "I'll tell you all about it when we meet." After a few more exchanges, we hung up, promising to meet up with the flawed.

Michael and I trudged through the deep snow and quickly entered the woods surrounding us. The forest was eerily quiet; all the life smothered out by the fresh layer of snow, and our footsteps seemed loud and intruding as we blundered past.

Suddenly I heard a noise, and I stopped. Michael turned in the direction, apparently hearing it as well.

I didn't even have time to open my mouth to suppose what it had been before I saw a pack of androids running through the trees.

Chapter Thirty-three

Guns. That was the only thing that registered in my mind. The androids had guns. I had lost mine back at the Institution, and I panicked inside, desperately wondering what we were going to do. I saw one of them raise their weapon, and I frantically shoved Michael out of the way, the bullet skimming my hair. I pushed him forward, and we ran.

The snow was hard to run through, and I hoped that would help us get away, rather than help the androids gain on us. We sprinted through the trees, the crunching of our shoes against the ground the only noise above our labored breathing. The snow seeped through my shoes, leaving a stinging sensation as well as a soggy one. I could feel Michael right beside me, and I was suddenly glad that he was now able to keep up.

I heard the androids behind us, along with the ringing sound of their pistol shots as they hit the trees and echoed throughout the forest. A few times I heard them alarmingly close, and I strove to pick up the pace.

We darted past trees and bushes, nearly falling a few times in the snow. After a few minutes I realized I could no longer hear the androids behind us, and I slowed slightly to look behind me. They were gone. I slowed to a stop and so did Michael. "Where did they go?" he asked nervously, looking around.

I was quiet, watching the trees.

Suddenly, out of nowhere, I heard a footstep and then something was being pressed to the back of my skull. "Don't move," a deep voice commanded, and Michael froze beside me. I heard the android take in a breath to say more, but before he had even uttered a sound, I had whirled around and knocked the gun from his hands. At the same time, Michael had grabbed the second android, taken his gun, and snapped the barrel in half with his fingers.

The android lunged for my neck, but I held him off. I kicked him hard in the shins, and he stopped momentarily in shocked pain. I took the opportunity, and we ran.

We sprinted across the snow, hearing angry shouts from behind us. I didn't wait to see if they were going to follow us, I just kept running.

Michael and I ran for about fifteen minutes before we finally slowed down to catch our breath. We looked around warily, expecting, but not hoping, to see androids stepping out of the trees. After a few moments of silence we concluded that we had lost them.

I breathed a sigh of relief. "They must have been left over from the attack on the camp," I said.

"Yeah," Michael replied, still scanning the area around us.

"Let's go," I said, and we hurried on. We half-walked, half-ran, for another ten minutes before we stopped again to look around. I surveyed the area, looking for any signs of people, when I heard noise and quickly turned in that direction.

"Drew!" I heard a voice exclaim quietly. I looked over and smiled to see Marian hurrying my way.

"Marian!" I replied. "Where are the others?"

"We're all spread out in groups around this area," she told me. "Come on." She beckoned for me to follow her. She glanced at Michael, and her eyes widened slightly. He smiled back, and she seemed to realize what had happened; her expression softened into one of ease. "Hi, Michael," she said with a grin. "Welcome back."

We walked a ways through the woods until we met up with a small group of about a dozen or so androids. I saw Jessica among them, and when she noticed us, she immediately jumped up and raced our way.

"Michael!" she cried, throwing her arms around him and hugging him. He hugged her back and then Jessica started gushing about how glad she was to see him.

We all waited around for Beatrix, Cassandra, Cameron, and Yvonne to show up, and they wandered in about an hour or two later, looking completely exhausted. They were all glad to see that I was okay, and they were gladly surprised to see Michael.

"So what happened?" Cassandra asked me once we had all settled around. "At the Institution?"

I explained to everyone how we had escaped, with a few gasps from Jessica at the part about the lethal injection. I briefly explained about what Glen had told me, leaving stunned looks on most of their faces. And then I recounted my encounter with the robot Drew, causing all of them to gape in horror and ask me multiple times if I was serious, to which I replied with a sober nod.

"What are we going to do?" Jessica asked slowly, a thoughtful but fearful expression on her face. "We can't let the creators do this." She cast us all a worried glance.

I was silent for a moment, a thought arising in my mind. One that would be dangerous, but seemed to be the only right thing to do. I looked around at all the others, and I suddenly saw in them the people who would help me accomplish what I needed to do. They had all gone through hard things in their lives, and their scars remained in their expressions, actions, and decisions. They all had been molded into survivors.

"Guys…" I said aloud, looking around at them. "We need to go back," I saw hope slowly slide into their expressions, "and finish what we started."

Chapter Thirty-four

We decided that we no longer needed a small operation; we needed a big one. A huge one. Most of the flawed had agreed to come, and all our weapons from camp were promptly retrieved and distributed. There wasn't enough to supply everyone with something, but there was enough to supply most of us.

The plan was relatively simple and a lot like our previous one. Yvonne would still hack the computers and some of us would still guard her. But the attack portion of our plan was different. We weren't sneaking in; there was no way we ever could. Instead, we were *breaking* in. We were going to force our way in even if it cost us our lives. We were going to go back to the Institution and finish everything once and for all.

There were no cars to take us all there, so we decided to walk. No one minded much. We were all fueled by anger and determination.

Yvonne walked alongside me, and I couldn't help but smile at the realization that Yvonne and I were finally on the same side. We weren't manipulating each other anymore. We were simply fighting for what we both believed in.

We seemed to reach the Institution sooner than we needed to. Something inside of me still told me that risking everyone's lives was pointless. But at the same time I was ready to end this. I couldn't wait any longer.

Guns raised and aimed, we barged through the Institution's front doors and into the lobby where a startled and bewildered creator sat at the desk. I couldn't help but smile at his expression upon seeing how many androids followed me inside. He opened his mouth to shout out, but one of the flawed had already knocked him out before he could even take a breath.

We marched past him and down the hallway leading toward the server room. We heard the thundering of footsteps that I used to dread, but now no longer feared. The androids rounded the corner, guns in hand, and Yvonne, a few others, and I sprinted away while a group of flawed held them back.

We reached the hallway to the server room, burst open the door, and hurried inside. I heard a shot and felt a bullet whiz by, but the creator who had fired was already out cold, Yvonne standing over him.

I ran to shut the door and heard androids hurrying down the hallway. I gripped my gun, not wanting to use it, but knowing that I would if I had to. It felt hot and dangerous in my hands, and I wanted to drop it, but I held on firmly.

Yvonne started typing away on the computer, and I could hear the shouts of androids and flawed outside of the room. I glanced around. Yvonne and I were the only ones in here, and she was steadily typing and clicking away, already done with the password and logging into the programming software.

I heard a bang on the door, and I jumped. Yvonne turned around but only for an instant before she was back to studying the computer screen. I heard the sound of a gun and jumped back as a bullet shot through the door. I immediately cocked my gun and shot at the bottom of the door, hoping to shoot the android's foot or leg and wound him. The bullet made sharp whizzing sounds as it collided and passed through the wood. I could almost sense Yvonne rolling her eyes at me. *You're weak, Drew,* she would say. And maybe I was. Or maybe I was brave to decide for myself that I would never kill a human being. Maybe the creators were weak for mindlessly killing others. Maybe bravery is the ability to fight your desires, not to prove how cruel you can be. A thought flew to my mind; a thought that had never occurred to me before because I had never considered it to be true. *Maybe I am brave.*

I heard a shout through the door. My heart was pounding, and I stayed to the side in case any more bullets flew through. I cast a glance at Yvonne, wondering how far she was and how long this would take her.

We had only been in here a few minutes, although it had seemed like hours. Through the door, I could hear the sounds of a battle going on. A battle that made me sick to my stomach. The sounds of bullets whizzing by and cries and shouts from androids and flawed all mingled together to create the noise of something terrible and ugly. Something the creators had created.

I partially opened the door to look around and saw dozens of androids and flawed, probably all of them, enclosed together in the hallway, shooting and fighting. One of the androids shot at me, and I raised my gun to shoot back, hitting her in the arm, and causing her to drop her weapon. I scanned the crowd for Michael and was relieved to see him in the far corner, wrestling a gun out of an android's hands. Jessica and Marian were standing back to back, shooting at anyone who came their way, and although I couldn't seem to spot Cassandra or Cameron, I knew they were most likely all right.

I shut the door and turned back to Yvonne. "How long?" I asked.

She shook her head, not looking away from the screen. "I'm not familiar with the software," she explained. "I need to figure it out before I can disable it."

It made sense, so I closed my eyes and prayed for patience. The minutes ticked by and seemed like hours. Every cry from outside the door made my heart bleed, thinking that it might be someone I loved. I knew I couldn't exit the room and leave Yvonne unguarded, so I merely stationed myself by the door and used my gun to guard off anyone who tried to enter.

Suddenly the sounds from outside stopped. There were no more shouts or gunshots. I thought about opening the door, but was afraid to, unsure of what I might meet.

"Drew," I heard Yvonne's voice from across the room. It was oddly quiet and almost shocked. "I did it."

I didn't know what I had expected this moment to be like. Had I expected to run around shouting and laughing? Had I expected to be hugging everyone and basking in our victory? I didn't know what I had assumed would happen, but I just stood there, silent. I was shocked. Had I not believed we would get this far? Had I never really envisioned what this might feel like? I stood there, staring at Yvonne, and she stared back at me. Suddenly a small smile crept into her features and Yvonne was grinning. "I did it," she repeated. "We did it."

I smiled back and ran to the door, Yvonne right on my heels. Outside was just as quiet as Yvonne and I had been a moment earlier. Androids stared around in confusion and the flawed watched them in shock. It was so strange to see a place that had been a battlefield only moments before morph into something so eerily peaceful and quiet.

I slowly stepped out into the hallway as if afraid I might break the spell if I walked too loudly. The air seemed thick and hot around us, as if left over by the battle. Many of the androids lay wounded on the floor and were being helped up. I saw a heap lying in the corner, and with a catch in my breath, I saw that it had the same auburn hair and blue eyes that I did. I noticed Michael glancing in the same direction and then turning to look at me. She had never been human, I reminded myself. Shutting down her programming had shut her off, as well.

I saw Jessica and Marian heading our way, wide smiles on their faces, radiating the glow of success. I saw Cassandra across the room, and although she looked bloody and disheveled, a large grin painted her features. I looked over to congratulate Yvonne, but before the first word even left my lips, someone had barged through the double doors at the end of the hallway, a large bang echoing throughout the corridor.

All heads turned in his direction as Glen stormed our way. His gun was raised. He was aiming at me. His eyes burned living hatred. I opened my mouth to say something but no words came. The gun was fired. I was too shocked to move. I stared at Glen, not even registering in my mind what had truly happened. The gun had been pointed at my head; I would die. But just then, a dark flash of something tall and beautiful pushed me to the floor right before the bullet whizzed past my ear and pierced her in the heart.

Chapter Thirty-five

Yvonne sank to her knees, her face oddly expressionless. I cried out her name although the sound of my voice didn't seem to reach my ears. I knew the flawed had reached Glen and taken his gun away but my eyes were glued on the girl in front of me.

The beautiful girl who had risked her life to save mine. Selfish Yvonne no longer seemed so selfish. I couldn't feel my legs; my body was shaking, but I somehow managed to reach her before she fell completely over. I gripped her shoulders, holding her up as she leaned her head against my arm. *Oh God, don't let her die,* I pleaded silently, tears sliding out of the corners of my eyes. Yvonne couldn't die. Yvonne was indestructible, undefeatable, but for the first time, I realized how truly vulnerable she was.

I sat on the ground as Yvonne stared up at me, her dark eyes alive with something I had never seen before. "Drew," she said, a smile playing on her lips. Suddenly she coughed; blood spilling out of the corners of her mouth, her smile gone.

"Yvonne," I replied, my voice choking. Her breathing was labored, and she closed her eyes momentarily, squeezing them shut as if that would dull the pain. "Why?" I asked quietly. "Why did you do it?"

A tiny grin melted into her expression, although her eyebrows furrowed in pain. Her eyes were bittersweet, something I didn't know Yvonne was capable of conveying until now. "Because I love you," she replied softly, and those three words shocked me more than anything else I had ever heard. "You're the little girl I grew up with," she added. "How could I not love you?"

I stared at Yvonne in surprise, the tears coming freely now. They slipped out of my eyes and dripped down my cheeks. A tear landed on Yvonne's face, and she weakly brushed it away. "You don't have to cry for me, Drew," Yvonne said. "It's not like I don't deserve to die this way," she said with a strained, almost painful laugh.

I shook my head, wishing Yvonne didn't believe that. Her breathing was slowing and her eyes were losing their light. Their beautiful light that I had seen sparkle so many times. The smiles were gone; we both knew her fate.

Yvonne looked up at me, her eyes hesitant yet determined; a searching look etched on her face. She looked reluctant, as if she wanted to think through her next statement but knew she had no time. There was a long pause. "Do you think He'd forgive me?" she asked so softly I wasn't sure if I had even heard it. The whisper of a question so unlike Yvonne, yet something that sounded so good in her voice. Something so natural; so beautiful.

I stared at her, surprised, but only for a moment. "Yes," I replied quietly, because I knew it was true.

She took in a shaky breath, her body shuddering against mine, struggling to hold onto the life she knew she was going to lose. She looked up, her dark eyes searching mine with a passion I had never seen before. "Would you?" Her voice was a whisper; a thought. Something spoken so softly but so clearly at the same time.

"Yes, Yvonne."

A small smile spread across her face, crinkling her nose and lighting up her eyes, and I suddenly realized I had never seen Yvonne smile; not this way. Her smile wasn't sneaky or mocking; it was true happiness I saw conveyed in her eyes. A happiness I had never seen on her before.

Yvonne had a beautiful smile.

I could hear the others around me shifting and watching us, but I only had eyes for Yvonne. The girl who had saved my life. The girl who had chosen to die for me. The least likely candidate. The friend who I had loved the most all along.

I stared into Yvonne's beautiful, dark eyes as they slowly lost their light forever, and she died in my arms.

Chapter Thirty-six

A loud crash echoed through the room, and my head turned toward the sound, still muddled and slow. A woman walked through the doors at the end of the hallway, nearly tackled to the ground by the surrounding androids. I saw Glen being held off to the side and the look of disgust that washed across his face once he saw her.

Suddenly I stood, feeling all the pent-up anger I'd been storing over the hours, months, and years the creators had their hold over me.

"Drew!" the woman called, as a few androids held her back. I noticed a few flawed among them, but mostly androids from the Institution. Androids that, now that their programming was gone, had realized what the creators truly did to them. I frowned, wondering why she knew my name or felt the need to call it out. I supposed that most the creators knew my name by now, though.

"You killed her!" I shouted, feeling anger burst through me. Fury at Glen for shooting Yvonne, but also fury at every single creator because of what they did together. All of them, each and every one, had a hand in the events that lead to Yvonne's death.

The woman faltered, but only momentarily, and as she neared me, I suddenly recognized her. The woman from the hotel – blonde and blue-eyed. She had been a creator – she had never quit – although I had suspected it for awhile. I opened my mouth to say something to her, anything at all, but she talked over me.

"We have to get out," she called. "The building's burning."

I froze, confused. "Burning?" I asked sharply.

She nodded vehemently.

"Somehow there's a fire."

I stared at her for a long moment. It was plausible that with all the commotion, all the fighting and breaking in, that a fire could have been started along the way. I was just about to ask her where the fire was, to prove it, when a loud crash shook through the hallway. I steadied myself against the wall just as the door to the server room beside me crashed down, smoke pouring out into the hallway. A few people cried out, taking steps back, and I knew the fire had to have been going for awhile to be crumbling the building to pieces around us. I turned back to the woman. "Get everybody out," I said and then looked around for Michael, Jessica, and the rest of the flawed. Now I understood why the air had seemed so warm. Heat was emanating from the walls now, smoke coating everything a dark gray. Michael and Jessica hurried toward me as I scanned for a safe exit. Just then the ceiling above us began to cave, sending plaster, and white dust crashing to the floor. I could see Cassandra and Cameron hurrying down the opposite hallway, and I hoped everyone else had gotten out as well. Jessica was tugging on my arm, but I couldn't tear my gaze from the cloud of smoke and plaster.

"Yvonne," I said quietly.

"I'm sorry, Drew," I heard Michael's voice in my ear. "I'm sorry." He grabbed my arm and pulled me along, and we ran in the direction of the hallway, nearly tripping over the fallen ceiling. This corridor was just as hot as the previous one, and even though we had all been perfected and our android bodies were stronger in so many ways, we were all beginning to cough on the smoke. I saw Cassandra up ahead waving us over, and I noticed a window large enough for someone to fit through. She climbed through just as we reached her, and we began to file out after her. Michael insisted on waiting for both of us to get out first, so I climbed through the tiny window, clinging to the side of the building before jumping the long gap to the ground. My ankles screamed on contact with the cement, but I gritted my teeth and hurried toward the road, looking back to make sure Jessica and Michael had come out safely. They hurried over to me and we staggered, coughing, out to the road to join the large group of androids huddled there. I scanned the crowd for the flawed that had come with us. Everyone but Yvonne. My heart stung at the realization. She was gone. Really gone. I looked back at the burning building – my enemy, the heart of so many of my fears, and yet, not too long ago, my home. I had spent my life there. Memories sprang through my mind—Yvonne and I as children running through the halls, playing hide and seek. Then later, wanting to do everything I could for the creators. And later still, realizing they were wrong, that everything in my life I had worked for, was so dangerously wrong. And here was the building I had spent my life in, burning to the ground in front of me.

I felt a hand on my shoulder and I turned, expecting it to be Michael, Jessica, or even one of the flawed, but was surprised to find that it wasn't. I stepped away, the blonde woman's hand falling from my arm. "Drew," she said quietly as if she didn't know what else to say.

"You're a creator," I stated coldly. At this point, it was an accusation that completely explained itself.

She winced slightly, but continued to meet my gaze. "*Was* a creator," she insisted.

I shook my head. "I saw you. In the hallways. And why else would you be here if you weren't still a creator?"

She paused momentarily, her mouth open as if to speak. "For you, Drew," she said finally, her bright blue eyes staring straight into mine.

I stared at her for a long moment, trying to understand. "For me?" I echoed, about to go on and accuse her of all the things the creators had done. But just then I stopped, still watching her. She began to smile. A hesitant smile that took it's time forming on her face. And suddenly everything seemed to fall into place in a matter of seconds. Images of the blonde-haired woman ripped through my mind; the day she found me at the hotel, when *she* dropped the key in my cell, when she darted away in the hallway only minutes earlier, the photo on Glen's desk – only now did I realize how close they were standing, how Glen had his arm thrown casually over her shoulder. Now I knew why the woman's eyes had always haunted me. Bright blue flecked with lighter shades of turquoise and emerald. My eyes. My mother's eyes.

"You're..." I began and she nodded. I stopped my mouth still open. For some reason, I couldn't say the words. They seemed too strange, too foreign. Too good?

"I did stop being a creator," the woman said. "For awhile. Glen," she shook her head, "your father, forced me to stay away. He was so angry after I left. He said he'd hurt you if I ever came back," she explained, answering the questions I hadn't even asked yet. "But when I heard about androids rebelling from the Institution, I came looking for you, hoping you were one of them. And then, after I saw you that day at the hotel, I knew Glen would stop at nothing to get you back. You, above all the others, were his proudest accomplishment. I wanted to protect you in any way I could, so I convinced him I had been wrong and that I wanted to come back and help like I did before." She shrugged. "And he believed me."

I stared at her, lost for words. I couldn't even register all the feelings coursing through me. It seemed so strange that only hours earlier I had been devastated that the family I had longed for my whole life had been Glen, a lying murderous creator. And now, my mother stood in front of me, showing me that my dreams weren't completely gone.

I stood there, motionless, aware of Michael, Jessica, and the other flawed all watching us, but for some reason, no words left my lips.

"Drew," my mother said slowly, a hesitant smile tugging at her lips. "Say something."

I paused, before opening my mouth. "Thank you," I said quietly. "For coming back."

She smiled, relief evident on her features, stepping forward, and before I knew it, her arms were around me, pulling me into a hug. I stiffened at first, unable to help myself; after all, she had been a *creator*. But slowly, I let myself be pulled into her embrace, hugging her back, because for the first time in my life, I felt like I belonged.

Chapter Thirty-Seven

I stared down at the gravestone and the pile of red roses that adorned it. Seeing Yvonne's name engraved upon the cold, gray stone seemed to make everything more real; permanent. She was really gone.

The Institution had burned to the ground, leaving no trace of anything that had been left inside – Yvonne included. But this headstone sat here, reminding us of who she had been.

I kept expecting to turn around and see her smiling at me, laughing at something I had done, or rolling her eyes in the way she always had. But this gravestone shoved reality into my face like a blinding light; I wouldn't see Yvonne again for a long, long time.

A breeze blew by, rustling the roses and their leaves and carrying their sweet scent across the cemetery. I stared down at the flowers, so like Yvonne and her personality. Their dark and dangerous beauty accompanied by the brave and surviving thorns. I saw Yvonne in those dark, red roses, and that's why they lay piled upon her grave site, representing the girl she had always been to me.

I stood there in the cold, completely alone in the cemetery as I stared at the frozen ground. I had already gone over every memory of Yvonne. I had thought about all the times we had betrayed one another and then I went back to when we had been so innocent, so small; loving each other because that's what friends do. I wondered how our friendship could have morphed into something so twisted, and I hoped that those last few seconds of her life had brought us back to our childhood, to the days when we really would have sacrificed our lives for each other. I knelt next to the stone and rubbed one of the petals between my fingertips.

"Goodbye, Yvonne," I whispered. There were no tears in my eyes. Maybe I was all cried out. Maybe I was tired of being sad. Or maybe I had accepted this and was ready to move on. Maybe I was brave enough to let Yvonne go.

I stood up and slowly walked away from the grave, leaving Yvonne's memory buried under the sunny, winter sky in the hopes that someday God would remember her.

Epilogue

It was as if the world had stopped spinning. Or resumed. Either analogy worked because everything had changed dramatically. All the Institutions had been destroyed in a matter of weeks, and people seemed to go on living in a daze. Day after day passed as we tried desperately to retrieve our lives and bring them back to a normal pace. Michael and Jessica reunited with their parents sometime during the chaos, finding them perfected, but now of sound minds. All of my other flawed friends tried to do the same and after a few weeks of scurrying and mayhem, most everyone had been reunited with the people they had loved.

I thought about my mother, how our lives had intertwined, and how I couldn't imagine living without her. It had been so strange at first, figuring out how to act around my mother – someone you should be so comfortable with, and I was just slowly learning who she was. I thought about Glen, everything we had gone through, and my heart ached. I knew Glen was locked up in jail somewhere, but I didn't want to go to him. At the moment, I never wanted to go to him. But I knew that someday I would. Someday I would ask him about my life; at the Institution, with Yvonne, becoming an android. I would talk to him about what he had done to me. I would ask him why he did it, and I would try to find a trace of something human, something lovable under his cold and controlling exterior. I would try to find the father I had longed for all my life.

* * * *

I stared out across the field of snow about a mile away from the flawed camp. In the fall it had been a barren wasteland of shrubs and tree trunks but now, with a blanket of snow covering every ugly flaw, the field was beautiful; perfect. I looked up at the sun, peeking out behind a heavy gray cloud, sending a ray of sunlight down to the frozen snow, and I wondered how God could create something so beautiful, so perfect, and how no one seemed to see it. I looked out across the sparkling snow, a forgotten smile on my lips. God had already created something perfect. Why had the creators striven to make it better?

I heard footsteps in the snow behind me, and I turned to see Michael heading my way. "There you are," he said with a smile, coming to stand beside me.

I grinned back. "I just took a walk." Michael watched me for a moment, and I couldn't help but smile as he leaned down to kiss me.

A realization dawned on me. A realization that seemed to lift a huge weight off of my shoulders and make my smile widen. As Michael wrapped his arms around me I realized that I never needed to be what Glen had set me up to become. I never needed to be more than Drew because I knew that God would make up the difference. Michael loved me. My friends loved me. My mother loved me. And God loved me. The way that I was; no different, no better. I smiled as I wondered how I could have never grasped such a small and important concept. That I was okay. That just being Drew was good enough.

That I didn't need to be perfect.

About the Author

Pauline C. Harris is now seventeen years old and has been writing since the age of eight. After self-publishing her first book at the age of fourteen, she moved on to write the Mechanical Trilogy. She loves reading science fiction and fantasy, and her main hobby, other than writing, is playing violin in various orchestras and quartets. Mechanical, Perfect, and Flawed are her first professionally published novels.

Twitter: @PaulineCHarris
website/blog: paulinecharris.wordpress.com
Facebook:https://www.facebook.com/pages/Mechanical/4048219762757
43?ref=hl

Other works by this author with Melange Books, LLC

Mechanical, Book 1 of the Mechanical
Perfect, Book 2 of the Mechanical

www.ingramcontent.com/pod-product-compliance
Lightning Source LLC
Chambersburg PA
CBHW051844170626
46807CB00003B/1347